GONE GHOST

XOE MEYERS - BOOK SIX

SARA C. ROETHLE

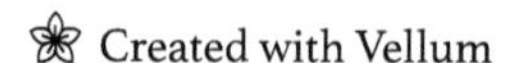
Created with Vellum

1

I placed the final clean dish into the dryer rack, then looked down at the dirty, soapy water in the sink. While I was glad to be living with my mom again, I wasn't thrilled to be back doing chores . . . especially now that the dishwasher decided to break.

I looked out my large kitchen window to the melting snow. The chilly Oregon winter had lasted long into spring, but it seemed it was finally letting up as sunlight danced across the ice in an almost dizzying display.

I glanced at the clock on the kitchen wall. Almost 9 am. Abel and Devin would arrive soon with our new pack members. Over the past six weeks, the decision had been made that instead of uprooting our small pack to join with a larger one, several other wolves would uproot their lives to join us. We were starting out with just two, but more would eventually come as each new person settled in. I had grudgingly accepted that I would still have to remain Alpha of the pack, since Abel believed having a demon in charge made us less likely to be attacked.

I wasn't sure I agreed with his logic. My presence hadn't stopped a group of rogue wolves from enlisting witches with the intent of wiping out my pack, less than two months before. I could finally admit that the witches had been mostly innocent, since they were only trying to stay alive, but their actions still led to my dad's death. Sure, my grandmother was really to blame, but she was dead. I needed someone of the living variety to be angry at, and the witches fit into that role nicely.

Of course, I hadn't seen any of them since I'd set fire to my father's corpse and returned to the demon underworld. They were all on the run from a demon they had foolishly summoned. Said demon had some sort of vendetta against them, and had already killed the coven's head witch, as well as the daughter of two coven members. If I crossed paths with the demon, I might try to send the fiend back underground, but I wasn't about to go out of my way to do anything concerning the witches.

I was pondering what type of demon the witches might be dealing with, when something hit the back of my head and kept pushing, shoving my face into the dishwater. The lukewarm water engulfed my entire head as the mini-wave created by my impact splashed down my chest. At first I was too surprised to act, but as whatever it was continued to hold me under, I began to thrash about, desperately seeking oxygen. Panicking, I braced my arms against the sink and kicked backward, but there was nothing there. I tried to use my sometimes supernatural strength to push myself away from the sink, yet whatever held me was incredibly strong and I didn't gain any ground.

As I struggled for a better grip on the counter, my hand met the dish rack and sent it flying to the floor. The clattering of breaking dishes was a distant echo as the water sloshed around my ears. I felt my lungs giving out, and knew I was only seconds away from inhaling dishwater and drowning. My last thought was that I would be forever known as the girl who drowned in her kitchen sink, then the pressure on the back of my head disappeared.

I reared back out of the water and collapsed to the slippery kitchen tile, sputtering for air as I searched for my attacker. There was no one there, but I could feel energy building in the room, like the feeling right before a storm broke. The kitchen lights began to flicker. At first it was just a few sporadic flashes, then the flickering grew more rapid until the bulbs simultaneously exploded with a starling *pop*. I ducked my head and covered my eyes in shock, then screamed as hands gripped me underneath my armpits and dragged me out of the kitchen.

I struggled, and was just about to burn whoever

had me, until the hands let go and I heard Jason's voice as he tried to calm me. I froze, then opened my eyes to look up at him through strands of my dishwater damp hair. He had let go of me to stand a few steps back, likely aware that he'd almost ended up a crispy vampire.

"What happened?" he asked breathlessly as he wiped the water from his hands onto his jeans. His dark blue eyes held concern as he approached and crouched in front of me while I remained huddled on the floor. He took in my wet hair and shirt, then glanced back over his shoulder to the kitchen and the broken dishes all over the floor.

"Something held me under," I wheezed, wrapping my arms around my knees to hold them to my chest. My legs didn't seem to want to work well enough for me to stand.

With a reassuring nod, Jason stood and left me to check the house for intruders. I watched his back, clad in a navy blue tee shirt, as he walked through the living room, then went upstairs. I would have helped him look, but I was still re-learning how to breathe.

He returned a few moments later and crouched in front of me. "There's no one else here. Did you see who it was?"

I shook my head. "They were gone as soon as they let me up, then all of the light bulbs exploded."

Jason offered me a hand and we both stood. Without the hand to support me I would have fallen.

Sensing my predicament, he retained his hold on me while he looked back at the kitchen again, deep in thought.

I wrung some of the water out of my hair with my free hand as I looked at him. "Not that I'm not grateful," I began, "but what are you doing here? I mean, I haven't really seen you much since we . . . "

"Broke up," he finished as he turned his gaze back to me.

The words still stung to hear, even though it had been my choice . . . mostly.

"Devin asked me to come," he explained.

"Why?" I pressed, beginning to feel more steady.

Jason shook his head as a knock sounded at the door. He looked me up and down. "I'll answer it if you want to get . . . cleaned up."

I nodded appreciatively, knowing that I likely had bits of food in my hair from the not very clean dishwater. I let go of his hand, then turned to head toward the stairs. I reached them and ascended quickly, chased off by the sound of Jason opening the front door. I hurried through my bedroom to the the adjoining bathroom, stripping off my damp shirt as I went.

As I stopped to stand in front of the mirror, I observed that I did in fact have food in my hair. I took a shaky breath, feeling almost fearful to turn on the faucet to wash it out.

I looked around the room cautiously, then turned the water on only enough to let out a gentle trickle.

With one more glance behind me, I flipped my hair over my head and draped it all into the sink. Once again silently chastising myself for not getting a haircut, I began washing sections of my white-blonde, shoulder blade length hair in the lukewarm water. The process was painfully slow, but I was still too shaken to run the water full-blast.

That done, I did my best at washing my arms, face, and chest in the sink, then grabbed a fluffy purple towel from the rack. I patted my skin dry, then wrapped my hair in the towel as I left the bathroom. Not wanting to waste any more time, I went through my closet, quickly donned a black, long-sleeve tee over my mostly dry jeans, then combed my fingers through my still wet hair. I grabbed the towel where I'd dropped it on the floor and tossed it onto my bed as I left the room, knowing the longer I took, the longer Abel's lecture would be for keeping him waiting.

I left my room and hurried downstairs, actually looking forward to a meeting I had been dreading, solely because after the kitchen experience, I really didn't want to be alone in the house.

I entered the living room to find Jason, Devin, and Abel, seated with two people I didn't know. The first new person was a girl who looked about my age, with dark skin and extremely curly, near-black hair. She looked frail, but in a healthy way, and I could tell that she was probably no more than 5'3", as her feet barely reached the ground from her perch on my cushy love seat. The other person was older, probably around fifty, and had dusky red hair framing her lightly lined face. She dressed like my mom, kind of conservative hippy, and her serene smile and kind green eyes made me like her instantly.

Abel and Devin both rose from where they sat beside the older woman on the couch to acknowledge me. I didn't see Jason, but I could smell coffee brewing and knew he must be in the kitchen. Better him than me. I wasn't planning on going back into the kitchen ever again, and it wasn't just to avoid doing the dishes.

Abel and Devin both wore suits. Devin looked comfortable, but Abel awkwardly straightened out his slacks as he approached. He was probably wishing he was in his normal attire, a vest with no shirt, or a tight tee shirt. His long, dark hair hanging loose around his striking features was the only hint of casual in his appearance.

"I trust you had a good reason for keeping us waiting?" he questioned as he took in my wet hair with his perceptive, hawk-like eyes.

I smiled sweetly. "You very well know that there's *always* a good reason for everything I do."

Jason entered the room and came to stand beside me with a tray supporting several mugs of coffee. "Someone tried to drown her in the kitchen sink," he explained, looking at Abel.

I gave Jason a sharp look.

"There really isn't a moment's rest with this one,"

Devin lamented as he ran his fingers through his pale blond hair, mussing its meticulously styled appearance. He winked one of his sky blue eyes at me as I glared at him.

I turned my attention back to Abel. Giving in to the fact that he would want more information, I held up my hands to stop him from speaking. "I didn't see who it was, and the light bulbs mysteriously exploded afterward. That's all I know."

Abel inhaled, then let out a long breath. He gestured back to the two women, who were staring at us like we'd all grown second heads. "Allow me to introduce Emma and Siobhan. I sincerely hope that I haven't brought them into a . . . situation."

He'd gestured to the younger girl as Emma, and the older woman as Siobhan. Both of them looked worried, though Emma much more so than Siobhan. Just judging by appearance, Siobhan didn't strike me as a woman that would get overly worked up by much.

"I'm sure it will be fine," I said patiently as Jason began handing out mugs of coffee. Everyone took one, except for Abel.

Once the coffee was doled out, I helped Jason move two extra chairs from the dining room to the living room so we would all have a place to sit. I ended up in one of the chairs, with Abel in the other, leaving Jason to sit with Devin and Siobhan on the couch. The hierarchy of the seating arrangement was obvious with Abel and I sitting taller than everyone else.

Abel glanced back and forth between my two new pack members. "Do either of you have any questions for Xoe?"

Emma raised her hand sheepishly. After Abel nodded for her to speak, she cleared her throat. "Do you go to high school? I'm supposed to start my senior year in the fall, and I'd really like to graduate."

I cringed. I'd come to terms with remaining a drop-out, even though I was living back in the human world. For me, there was just no going back.

"I don't," I replied, not bothering to explain my situation, "but Lucy does. She's another member of the pack, and I'm sure she'd be more than happy to get you settled in."

Emma nodded to herself as Siobhan focused her gaze on me enough to make me uncomfortable. Intelligence radiated from her eyes as she sized me up, then raised her hand to speak.

"What do you expect from your pack members?" she asked before Abel could call on her. I was startled by her southern accent, especially with her Irish name.

I narrowed my eyes at her in confusion. "I'm not quite sure what you mean."

"Well, I've never had a demon Alpha before," she explained. "Do the rest of the pack members still shift together? What are we supposed to do for you?"

I was still confused by her line of questioning. What were they supposed to *do* for me?

"Um," I began, wracking my mind for something to

say, "I know Lucy and Max sometimes shift together, so you could probably join them if you want to. Lela tends to keep to herself, and we all try to respect that."

Her eye twitched at the latter part of my explanation, though whether it was the mention of Lela, or that she liked to keep to herself, I wasn't sure.

"And what about my other question?" she replied without missing a beat.

I felt myself blush and I wasn't sure why. Part of me wanted to order her to lay daily offerings at my feet and dance naked in the moonlight, but something told me that Siobhan was not a woman that appreciated being messed with.

"Protect each other?" I said like it was a question.

Siobhan narrowed her eyes, trying to discern whether or not I was being genuine. "You're not like any Alpha I've ever known," she said finally.

I shrugged, not knowing what else to say. The silence began to draw out as we all stared at each other.

"Well," Devin said with a sudden clap of his hands. "I think it's time to get Siobhan and Emma settled into their new home. You can work out your pack . . . dynamics later. The leaders need to have a meeting."

I looked a question at Devin, unaware of any "meeting" besides the awkward one we'd just had. I stood and shook both of the women's hands as they rose, then Devin ushered them out the front door. All three of them left mostly empty mugs of coffee behind. I looked down at my own mug of coffee still clutched in my left hand, then set it down on the coffee table with the others. Coffee and nervous stomach knots simply don't go together.

Abel and Jason had stood with the rest of us, and now returned to their seats. I took one glance at the empty chair beside Abel, then took the empty love seat instead.

"First thing's first," Abel said as he turned to look at Jason. "I have a job for you."

It wasn't the first thing I'd expected to hear, or the middle, or the last, for that matter. Logically, I knew that Abel had hired Jason's services before. Heck, it was how I'd met Jason in the first place, but it seemed like Abel liked having Jason around my little pack. One more scary monster to ward off the bad guys. Would he really choose to send him away now?

My anxious string of thoughts was interrupted as Jason gestured for Abel to continue.

"I was hoping to hire you to watch over Emma," he explained. "She has an abusive father, and I'm worried that he might come looking for her."

"Is her father a werewolf?" Jason asked.

Abel shook his head. "Human, but dangerous."

The thought of Emma with an abusive father gave me chills, and I was suddenly very glad that she had been chosen as one of my new pack members. She seemed so small and helpless. I would just pass off the gratitude that I felt upon learning that Jason wouldn't be chasing some rogue wolf somewhere far away as gratitude that we would get the chance to keep Emma safe. I was grateful for both, but the Jason side of things made me feel weak and pathetic. He wasn't *mine* to keep around.

"Sounds simple enough," Jason replied after a moment of thought.

Abel nodded and handed a piece of paper to Jason. "This is the address of where Emma will be living. I know you'd rather not harm a human, so if he shows up, have Xoe do it."

"Hey!" I exclaimed, taking instant offense at what he'd said. "I'd rather not harm a human either."

Abel grinned at me, and I realized too late that he was pulling my leg. Before I could say something scathing, he asked, "What do you think of your new pack members?"

I shrugged. "They're not what I expected, but they seem nice."

Abel raised a dark brow at me. "What do you mean, *not what you expected*?"

I shrugged again. "Well the whole idea is to make the pack larger and therefore more intimidating. I just assumed that the new wolves themselves would be large and intimidating."

Abel nodded. "I had considered that, but at the end of the day, Emma and Siobhan are more likely to accept a teenage girl as their leader than some of our more formidable wolves."

"Because they're women?" I prompted.

Abel had the grace to look slightly embarrassed. "That, and neither of them are terribly dominant, though Siobhan may pretend to be. It will make for an easy transition, hopefully free of power struggles. There may be men among the next group of new pack members. The only qualification is that they must be less dominant than you."

Jason snorted. "I don't imagine you'll have much trouble finding plenty of wolves that fit that particular bill."

I turned toward Jason and scowled. "Just what is that supposed to mean?"

He gave me a good-natured smile. "Don't be modest, Xoe. I've never seen you back down to *anyone*."

He'd meant the words in a joking way, but I could sense some bitterness behind them. We had, after all, broken up because of that very personality trait.

I took a deep breath and let the line of questioning go. "So where will they live? Is Emma even old enough to be on her own?"

"Siobhan is Emma's guardian," Abel explained. "Emma's father lost custody when her mother died. He's an addict with multiple convictions. Siobhan has been a foster parent for many years, and she's helped to raise many young wolves left without parents, so it was only natural that Emma go to her."

"But her dad has refused to leave the picture entirely?" I prompted.

Abel answered with a curt nod. "We've done our

best to keep him away thus far, but he has eluded our grasp."

I laughed bitterly. "I imagine the *grasp* to which you are referring would come with some very sharp claws."

Abel nodded again, this time with a secretive smile.

I smirked. "Is this whole foster parent thing even legal?" I asked skeptically, mainly because I wasn't sure how Abel would have otherwise managed to make sure that wolf children didn't end up with human foster parents.

Abel chuckled to himself. "Emma was placed with Siobhan by the state of California, and the state also permitted their move to Oregon." When I raised an eyebrow at him, he added, "You're not the only one with friends in high places."

I squinted at him. As far as I was aware, *he* was the only one with friends in high places. "I don't follow," I admitted.

"Well, you have *me*," he explained, "and word on the street is that many of the upper demons are beginning to take an interest in you."

My mood instantly soured. "The last two upper demons that took an interest in me are dead. Three, if you include my father."

Abel bit his lip, and judging by his expression, if he was a little more flexible he would have lifted his foot into his mouth. "I didn't mean to bring up any hurtful subjects," he said evenly.

I shrugged and shelved the pain of my father's

death and my grandmother's betrayal to the back of my mind, where it had been resting and gathering dust for the past several weeks.

"Okay," I sighed after a moment. "I assume we've gone over everything? I'll introduce Emma and Siobhan to the others, and Jason will make sure that Emma's dad doesn't come near her?"

"That's correct," Abel stated as he stood. "Devin and I will wait in town for another week or so, just to make sure we don't have any more . . . mishaps. Then you will be on your own."

"Peachy," I replied, actually not looking forward to things getting back to normal. At least with the constant drama, I didn't have to deal with being a jobless, fatherless, high-school drop out.

Abel shook Jason's hand as Jason stood, and I stood and offered my hand as well. At first I thought Abel was going to snub me, but then he leaned in and pulled me into an uncomfortable hug.

"I truly am sorry about your father," he said softly as he patted my back lightly.

A moment later, the embrace was over and he headed for the door without another word. I scrunched my eyebrows at Jason in confusion.

He shrugged in reply as Abel shut the door behind him.

Jason and I had a moment of awkward silence before he said, "I suppose I should go find Emma, but . . ."

"But . . . " I pressed.

Jason sighed. "I know it's not my place, but I'd rather you not be alone after what happened in the kitchen."

My heart sped a little at the recent memory. Honestly, I didn't want to be alone either, but I couldn't ask Jason to stay with me. I had somewhere to be. "I promised Dorrie I'd visit today, so I won't be alone. Maybe I'll go to the demon library and look up invisible beasties that try to drown people in dirty dishwater."

"You can just tell me you're going to see Chase," Jason stated bluntly.

My mouth dropped at his accusation. Sure, I *was* planning on seeing Chase, but I really had promised Dorrie a visit.

"He's still looking for Sam," I replied, "and I can poof us around the underground much faster than Chase can run." Okay, maybe I was making up excuses. True excuses, but excuses none-the-less.

"I really don't think he believed your grandmother would hurt either of you," Jason said sadly. "Maybe you should just let him go."

I felt a wash of anger, but forced it back down. "He may not have believed it, but he still tricked us. That trick cost my father his life. Sam will pay for that, if nothing else."

Jason shook his head. "Okay, I'm sorry for bringing anything up. It really isn't my place."

"You're entitled to your own opinions," I assured, though the scowl I felt on my face probably didn't help to back up my words.

Jason put his hands in his pockets and gave me a long, searching look. I wasn't sure what he found, but with another sigh he announced, "I'll go find Emma. Let me know when you're ready to introduce her to Lucy and the others."

I nodded. In the blink of an eye, Jason was gone, and the door was shut and locked behind him. I took a few steps forward and glanced into the kitchen to find Jason had cleaned up the water and broken dishes while I was in the shower. The light bulbs had been replaced as well, and there wasn't a hint of glass from their explosions. What I wouldn't give to be able to clean with supernatural speed and multitasking abilities.

I looked at the clock to see that I still had a good five hours before my mom would get home from work. I wasn't sure if whatever had attacked me would go after her, but better safe than sorry. My visit to the underground would have to be a short one. Dorrie would be disappointed. Chase probably would too . . . so would I, but don't tell anyone. It will be our little secret.

2

I arrived in my dad's kitchen accompanied by a whoosh of red smoke. I looked around for signs of life, fanning my hand in front of my face to clear the air. The smoke didn't actually have a smell to it, but it obscured my vision for a few seconds after I popped into a different place.

I watched the last of the smoke clear with a scowl. It was too big of a coincidence that I'd only learned to *travel* after my dad and grandmother were both dead. It was suspicious, to say the least. Then again, maybe it was just a trait passed on by death. Stranger things had happened. They happened to me on an almost daily basis.

I left the kitchen in search of Dorrie and Chase, secretly hoping I'd find Chase first. I wanted a moment alone with him. My wish was not granted, as I reached the first room and found Dorrie mixing something at my dad's alchemy table.

My heart hurt a little to see all of the things my dad had last touched moved around and getting used up, but it was good that Dorrie had found a hobby. I'd stolen her from her previous life, and it was the least I could do for her.

The normally tidy room was strewn with open books and crumpled up pieces of paper. There were also a few new burn marks in the carpet around the alchemy table. In the center of all the chaos was Dorrie, translucent hair tied back to reveal her glittery white neck and ears. She turned her crystalline blue eyes toward me to display soot marks on her face and her white tee shirt.

She'd recently started wearing normal clothes instead of the white jumpsuit she'd worn as a driver, but her jeans and tee shirt made her look even more strange in contrast. Chase had gotten the clothes upon her request, since she had a larger frame than me and couldn't fit into any of my hand-me-downs.

"Pop Tart!" she exclaimed as she stood to wrap me in a scratchy hug.

Her body felt hard and hollow, and I knew for a fact that it was, since I'd seen her shattered several weeks before. Her broken parts had remained where we left them in the bathroom, even after she'd been re-formed, unbeknownst to us, back in the dream realm. She'd passed it off as her being a construct of demon magic, but it still confused the heck out of me.

"I need more library books," she announced as she released me.

"We'll have to return all of these first," I said, gesturing to the books littering the floor. "And I'm pretty sure you've read all they have on alchemy."

Dorrie nodded excitedly. "I know, I want history books now. Demon ones *and* human ones."

I raised an eyebrow at her, waiting for an explanation.

"I just find it all so fascinating!" she exclaimed. "I was never allowed to learn new things as a driver. I was to remember where to go, and that was *it*."

"Whatever floats your boat," I conceded with a smile.

Dorrie smiled back, "It does float my boat, it floats my boat very much."

I laughed. I had to hand it to Dorrie, she always put me in a better mood. "Where's Chase?" I asked, unable to wait any longer.

Dorrie frowned. "Looking for Sam. He got another lead, but I imagine it will be fruitless like all the others."

"He wasn't supposed to go looking without me," I sighed.

Dorrie tilted her head to the side and gave me a sympathetic smile. "You'll find that little rat soon enough, Dumpling. I want him to pay too."

"Yeah," I replied, nodding to myself. "So do you want me to go to the library first, or do you want to play some Checkers?"

"Checkers!" Dorrie shouted in excitement, just as I knew she would. She had become obsessed with the game, enough so that she beat me almost every time. I would feel little sadness when she finally got tired of it.

We went into the den where the board was already set up on the coffee table from our last game. I sat reluctantly on the cushy leather sofa while Dorrie curled up on the floor on the opposite side of the board.

As we played I told her about my morning, and the unfortunate incident with the kitchen sink.

"Sounds like you're being haunted," she commented, like it was perfectly normal.

"Haunted?" I questioned. "Like ghosts?"

Dorrie smirked at me. "You're a demon who hangs out with vampires and werewolves, and you don't believe in ghosts?"

I shrugged. "Well I can *see* the vampires and were-wolves . . . " I trailed off, thinking back to Sam's little harem of spirits. I *had* seen those ghosts, and I had felt them too as they carried me to a cell in the human world, right where my grandmother had wanted me.

Dorrie laughed. "Ghosts are really common in the dreamworld, and in lots of the other realms. Most of them are harmless though. Maybe a particularly powerful one tagged along with you when-" she cut herself off abruptly.

"When my grandmother died," I finished for her. "That's the last time I was in the dreamworld." I had a sickening realization. "Right before we left, I remember something hitting me in the back. It felt like someone shoved me, but there was no one there."

"You don't think your granny . . . " she trailed off.

My eyes widened. "Is it possible? Whatever attacked me this morning tried to drown me in the sink. I wouldn't be surprised if my grandmother wanted a little vengeance."

"Oh Snickerdoodle," Dorrie said softly, "this is *bad*."

I gazed off as I thought things over. "But if it was my grandmother," I said finally, "why did she let me go?"

Dorrie shrugged. "Maybe she lost her connection. Maybe you somehow booted her back to where she came from."

I shook my head. I didn't think that was it. I had been about to lose consciousness, and really didn't think I was capable of exorcising a ghost at that moment. I began to feel anxious as I thought of the possibilities of my grandmother hanging around in ghost form.

"Do you think she'll try to hurt anyone else?" I asked, suddenly horrified that everyone I cared about was in a different place at that moment.

Dorrie wrinkled her brow in thought. "If she

hitched a ride, you're probably her only connection to this world. She might try to hurt others around you, but other than that, I don't think she would be able to."

"So my mom will be safe in the house as long as I'm not there?" I pressed.

Dorrie nodded. "Maybe you ought to stay down here for a while. She can't drown me since I don't need air, and you and Chase can watch out for each other."

I sighed. It wasn't a bad idea. Of course, Dorrie could be wrong about everything, and maybe my mom's house just had a poltergeist.

The front door opened and shut, startling me. Lost in the subject at hand, I had forgotten for a moment that we were waiting for Chase to get home.

A few seconds later he found us in the den. Staying seated, I glared up at him.

"What?" he asked as he nervously raked his fingers through his near-black hair. His dark gray eyes wouldn't meet mine, letting me know that he knew exactly what the glare was about. He straightened his neutral-colored flannel over his faded, gray jeans as he waited for me to speak.

"You weren't supposed to go without me," I chided.

He came to sit beside me on the couch. His nearness raised my pulse a few notches, as was per usual of late. Things had been strange since we'd had our second kiss, but had decided not to date. Well, I had decided. It seemed like a bad idea to enter into a new relationship right on the tail of the last one. Not to mention that my life was in total shambles. I needed to figure some stuff out before I could be with *anyone*. Of course, logic couldn't stop the nervous pitter patter of my heart, just as it couldn't stop my constant over-thinking of, well, *everything*.

"I had a time-sensitive lead," he explained, oblivious to my inner monologue, "and you had your meeting with your new pack members. I really had no choice," he finished as he batted his eyelashes at me sarcastically. "How was the meeting by the way?"

I shrugged, still angry. "As good as could be expected. Siobhan and Emma both seem nice. Emma is around my age."

"Tell him what happened," Dorrie insisted, before I could get to it.

I scowled at her, then turned back to Chase. "Something tried to drown me in my kitchen sink."

Chase's eyes widened. "Come again?"

"We think her grannie hitched a ride from the dreamworld," Dorrie cut in, "and now she wants vengeance."

Chase looked at Dorrie, then turned back to me with an astonished expression. "You'd think you would have led with that."

"We don't know that it was my grandmother," I explained uncomfortably. "but something invisible shoved me before we left the dreamworld, and now something invisible tried to drown me."

Chase shook his head. "Now we *really* need to

find Sam."

"Why?" I said, not comprehending his train of thought.

Chase rolled his eyes at me. "He has control over the dead, Xoe."

My mouth opened into an *oh* of understanding. "He's going to have a hard time trying to control my grandmother with me throwing fireballs at him. He'd probably have a hard time of it regardless. She was powerful in life, and I've no doubt that if this is in fact her ghost, she'll be just as powerful in death."

"He's our best bet without-" he cut himself off. People were doing that around me a lot lately.

"Without my father," I finished for him. "Normally we'd be running straight to him with this kind of problem."

Chase glanced at me, then quickly looked away. Dorrie watched us with intense interest like a little kid watching her parents have a conversation that she didn't quite understand. She knew that I was still mourning my dad's death, but she still didn't comprehend the need for tact when discussing said death. I actually appreciated her bluntness. Everyone tip-toeing around me was starting to get annoying.

"Maybe you should stay down here until we figure this out," Chase said finally.

Dorrie nodded excitedly in agreement.

"I'm supposed to introduce the new pack members to the old ones," I argued. "They might get a little concerned if I just disappear."

Chase sighed. "Is Abel still in town? Maybe he knows a witch . . . one that isn't on the run from a throat-tearing demon."

I shook my head. "I've had my fill of witches for a few life-times."

Chase gave me a sympathetic look. "If we can't find Sam, a witch might be our only shot. It's probably not a good idea to wait around for it to happen again."

I shrugged. "Well I stopped it somehow. Or something did. Maybe we should wait for it to happen again so we can figure out if it was something I did."

"Then I'm coming above-ground with you," he stated, his face making it clear that there would be no arguments.

I snorted. "I could just poof out of here right now and leave you," I jested.

Chase frowned. "Please don't make me explain to your mother why she had to find your dead body face down in the toilet."

I punched his arm. "It was the kitchen sink!"

He waggled his eyebrows at me. "*This* time."

I scowled back at him, but he was right. I didn't want my mom to find my dead body in her house, or anywhere for that matter. My life might have been in total shambles, but I didn't want to die. Still, I felt oddly numb about the whole situation. So many monsters had been out for my blood lately that it was becoming commonplace. That thought alone was enough to make me want to ask Abel if he knew any witches. Mortal peril shouldn't be commonplace.

Dorrie stared at me and read my expressions as I thought things over. When I stood with a nod, she jumped to her feet.

"Please get my library books before you leave!" she exclaimed. "It's *so* boring when both of you are gone."

I cringed, because I had completely forgotten about her library books.

Chase stood and patted my back. "I'll get them if you promise not to leave without me."

I held up my hand in the salute for *scout's honor.* With a nod of acceptance, Chase followed Dorrie out of the room while she explained to him the types of books she wanted.

I slouched back down onto the couch and let out a breath, knowing that it would probably be my last moment of alone time until we figured out the whole haunting situation. Sure enough, a minute later Dorrie came bounding back into the room to resume her seat on the other side of the Checkers board.

"Chase says I'm not to let you out of my sight until he gets back, Apple Pie," she began as she cleared the board to start a new game, "so I hope you don't mind company when you go to the bathroom."

I rolled my eyes. "I don't think that's what he meant."

Dorrie sat up straight and stared me down with her twinkling blue eyes. "Since your daddy isn't around anymore, the job of protecting you falls to me and Chase. I'm not about to fail on my half of the responsibility."

I squinted my eyes at her and tried to think of where she might have gotten this new idea from. "Did Chase tell you that . . . about protecting me, I mean?"

Dorrie looked at me like I was being silly. "Of course not, Pop Tart. That's what your daddy told me before he left that day."

My mouth dropped in astonishment. Had my dad known he was in danger? I would have given a lot in that moment to know what my grandmother had told him to trick him into meeting with Sam. He obviously didn't know at the time that my grandmother was the real threat, else he wouldn't have trusted her. So the question was, what was my father trying to protect me from?

"Did he say anything else?" I asked urgently.

Dorrie shook her head sadly. "I'm sorry, Bon-Bon. I didn't mean to upset you."

I shook my head. "No," I replied distantly. "You've just given me a few things to think about."

Placated, Dorrie moved her first checker piece. I followed suit, not really thinking about what I was doing. I thought back to the file Sam had left on our doorstep, a file of information about our ancestry that my dad had been gathering. I didn't see what it had to do with anything, or why it might make him fear for his life.

We really needed to find Sam. He might even survive the encounter. Then again, he might not.

3

By the time Chase returned from the library, Dorrie had beaten me at Checkers three more times. At the sight of the huge stack of books in his arms, Dorrie hopped up from her seat, leaned down to give me a quick, scratchy hug goodbye, then hurried over to take the books from Chase. With her new prizes in hand, she left the room, presumably to return to my dad's alchemy room.

"Are you ready to go?" Chase asked as I cleaned up the Checkers board.

I nodded and stood. "There's something I need to tell you first."

He crossed his arms and smiled at me. "What *now*?" he asked sarcastically.

I looked down at my sneakers nervously, trying to figure out how to tell him that Jason had been hired by Abel to watch over Emma. If Chase showed up with me when I introduced my new pack members to the old ones, things would likely be highly awkward between him and Jason, and that would make things awkward for me.

Yet, as I thought about what I should say, it dawned on me that it really wasn't my responsibility to say anything. I wasn't dating either of them. They were adults, and if they wanted to have awkwardness, that was up to them.

"Xoe?" he questioned, sounding worried after I'd been silent for so long.

I finally met his gaze with a small smile. "Nothing," I stated. "Let's go."

Chase looked unsure as I held my hand out to him, but finally he took it. We stood there for a moment while I thought about how nice his hand felt in mine, then I closed my eyes and thought of home.

We were there in an instant, standing in a faint cloud of red smoke. Chase let out a sigh of relief; this new mode of travel was exceptionally more comfortable for my passengers. I hadn't made a portal since I'd discovered how to travel properly, and I didn't miss the dizzying feeling of rushing upward, nor did I miss the destruction my portals caused. At this rate I'd never figure out why my portals had been so wonky, and I was okay with just letting it go if it meant I wouldn't ruin my mom's house again.

I left the living room where we'd appeared to glance at the clock in the kitchen. I didn't actually go *into* the kitchen though. I'd never thought to see the day that I'd be afraid of a kitchen sink, but there it was. Big, bad half demon afraid of a little water.

I retreated and turned back to Chase. "We still have an hour until Lucy and Max are home from school. Shall we make some lunch?"

Chase nodded. He walked toward the kitchen, then stopped when I didn't follow. "I thought you said you wanted lunch?" he said like it was a question.

I cringed. "What I really meant was, will you make lunch? I'm still feeling a little kitchen-phobic."

Chase sighed in an exaggerated manner. "I *suppose*, but while I do that, you can call Abel and ask if he knows any *trustworthy* witches."

I glared at him. "I'm pretty sure the term *trustworthy witches* is an oxymoron."

Chase smirked at me. "If you want lunch, you have to call him."

"But I already had to see him once today," I whined.

"Call him," Chase stated again as he disappeared into the kitchen.

"Fine!" I shouted. "But I'm going to need some coffee first!"

I was answered by the sound of beans being ground in the coffee grinder. I sat down on the couch to wait with absolutely no intention of actually calling Abel. Several minutes later Chase joined me with two turkey sandwiches and two cups of coffee, arranged neatly on my mom's serving tray. He sat on the couch and placed the tray between us, then picked up his sandwich without a word.

He paused his eating to take a sip of his coffee, then glanced up at me.

"What?" I asked, fearing that he was going to push me again to call Abel.

He put down his sandwich and cup, giving me his full attention. "I think I'm going to move out of your father's house," he stated bluntly.

I dropped my sandwich back to its plate in surprise. "I don't understand. You don't like living there? I mean, I know it's different now, but-"

He held up his hands to calm me down. "It's not that I don't like living there. It's just that . . . well, I was living there because I was working for your dad, and it just made things easier. Now that he's . . . gone, I need to find another job."

"And another house . . . " I prompted.

Chase cringed and shook his head, obviously not thrilled with the way the conversation was going. He reached out across the tray and took both my hands in his. "*Look*. It's *your* house now. He left it to you, and you should be able to do with it what you want."

"B-but I don't want to do anything with it," I stammered.

"And that's fine," he said soothingly. "It's just that now, after everything, it feels like I'm squatting in my friend's house. There is no purpose to me being there."

"Is this some sort of macho thing?" I asked as I

pulled my hands from his. "You could live there when my dad owned the house, but not when your younger, female demon friend owns it?"

Chase rolled his eyes again. "You know that's not why, Xoe."

"Then tell me *why*."

Chase picked up his cup of coffee, took a deep breath and let it out, took a sip, then met my eyes. "I told you once that I don't remember my father. I just know he was a Necro-demon, like Sam."

I wasn't sure what Chase's father had to do with our conversation, but since I'd been trying to get him to open up about his past since I first met him, I kept quiet and nodded.

"My mother was a Naga," he went on, "and I took after her."

This was more information that I knew. I'd once seen Chase kill a vampire by biting her. It was kind of ironic really. She had bitten him too, but Chase's bite was poisonous.

I nodded for Chase to go on, giving him my full attention.

"My parents were only together in order to procreate," Chase explained. "They each wanted a child to carry on their lines, and after I was born, they each had that. My mother took me, my father took Sam, and that was the end of it."

"That's horrible," I commented before I could think better of it.

Chase shrugged and took another sip of his coffee. “It's a common practice amongst demons. My mother was killed by another demon when I was fifteen,” he went on, speaking blandly about the event like it didn't hurt him, though I was sure that it did. “Sam found me shortly after. I didn't even know about him, but his spirits told him about me. He got me into quite a bit of . . . trouble. Then I met your dad. He helped me out, and in return asked me to watch over his daughter who was living in the human world.”

He shrugged again, brushing off the whole story. “I'd never had much of a purpose, but working for your dad gave me that. Now I need to find something else.”

“So you don't want to watch over his half-human daughter anymore?” I asked jokingly, trying to lighten the situation.

Chase smiled sadly. “I want to watch over her very much, but she is often quite busy, and I don't want looking for Sam to be my only day job.”

“I understand,” I said hesitantly, “but what about Dorrie?”

He sighed. “I thought about that. I'm still more than happy to be on Dorrie library duty.”

I smiled and picked up my sandwich again, but paused to look at him before taking a bite. “Chase,” I began, not sure how to phrase the question I wanted to ask.

He waited patiently while I figured it out, sipping his coffee and watching me with his calm, gray eyes.

"You said that what happened with you and Sam was a common practice amongst demons, but my powers are the same as my dad's. Why did he leave me?"

I suddenly felt like I was going to cry, and I really, *really* didn't want to cry. I'd cried enough.

Chase took my hand again and waited for me to meet his gaze. "He tried to stay and raise you in the human world at first, but when your mom ran away with you, he decided it was for the best. He wanted you to be able to live a normal life for as long as possible. He didn't want your life like it is *now* to be the only kind of life you'd ever know."

I sighed and looked away. "I wish I could have known him all of that time." Before Chase could reply, I shook myself out of my fugue. "Sorry about your mom," I said quickly. I looked back up at him. "Thanks for telling me."

Chase nodded. "Now eat your sandwich. You need to call Abel so we can figure this haunting thing out."

With my focus on Chase's past, and my dad, I had forgotten about calling Abel, and had nearly even forgotten that I was being haunted. The reminder instantly soured my mood. My phone buzzed in my pocket. I fished it out, thinking that Lucy had texted me back, but what I found was a text from an unknown number. It read:

"Meet at *Mountain Heights* apartments, #201. You said you would help if you could."

I stared at the text in confusion for a moment, then showed it to Chase.

"Well you're not exactly *helpful*," he commented. "There are only so many people that it could be."

I glared at him, then typed, "Who is this?"

I pushed send, then tapped my foot impatiently while I waited for a reply. A moment later my phone buzzed again.

"Please help."

I showed the message to Chase.

"Well my curiosity is piqued," he admitted.

"Aaand our day just got a little longer," I replied.

My phone buzzed again, and this time it actually was Lucy, replying that she would gather Max and Lela to meet me and the new pack members at Irvine's in an hour.

I showed the text to Chase. "Looks like we don't have time to call Abel," I said with an evil smile.

"Xoe-" he began to argue, but I ignored him and sent a text to Jason asking him to bring Emma and Siobhan to Irvine's.

Surely with such a large party as a buffer, Chase, Jason, and I would be fine?

"*Xoe*," Chase stated again. "Your life being in danger needs to take priority here."

I shrugged. "My life is always in danger."

Chase shook his head. "Not like this."

I met his earnest eyes and was forced to answer him seriously. "I think the anonymous text was probably from Rose, Claire's little sister," I admitted. "If that's the case, we already have a meeting with witches set up. I wouldn't exactly say that they're of the *trustworthy* variety, but they want my help, and will likely be inclined to help me in return."

Chase let out a sigh of relief. "Why didn't you just say that to begin with?"

I looked down at my lap. "Because I hope that the text wasn't from Rose. It would mean they want help with the demon the witches loosed, the one that killed Claire."

"*And*?" Chase prompted.

I took a deep breath. "And I'm not sure that I want to help them."

Chase looked slightly confused. "You know they had little choice in what they did. Your grandmother was controlling them."

"Would you sacrifice an innocent person's life to avoid risking your own?"

Chase shook his head. "They didn't think of it as risking innocent humans. They thought of it as risking demons. As far as the witches are concerned, demons are evil."

I snorted. "So I'm back to asking myself why I should help them. If demons are evil, I should leave the witches to their fate."

Chase moved the sandwich tray to the coffee table so he could scoot over and put an arm around me. "You'll help them because *you* are not evil, Xoe."

"What makes you so sure?" I asked seriously, because truth be told, I was a little worried.

I had only ever tried to harm those who had harmed me, but did I mourn their deaths? Not one bit. I was more inclined to help Rose and her parents, not because it was the right thing to do, but because they could help me in return. I really didn't want anything bad to happen to Rose, but to her parents? They had it coming.

"What are you thinking?" Chase asked, instead of answering my question.

"That I hope the demon gets to Ben and Cynthia before I have a chance to stop it," I answered honestly.

"They were only trying to help their daughter," Chase replied.

"Well they should have thought of their children before they went around summoning demons to begin with," I countered. "They made a choice. They could have left their coven and moved away from the rogue wolves who were threatening them. They could have reported it all to the coalition. Instead, they made a choice that cost their daughter and my dad their lives. They decided to play with fire, and they deserve to get burned."

Chase smiled sadly and pulled me a little closer. "You are very much like your father."

"What does that mean?" I asked, letting my head fall against his shoulder.

"You're highly moral, but it's your own form of

morality. An eye for an eye, reap what you sow, old-school kind of morality."

"I don't think wanting someone to die can really be considered moral," I argued.

"You want them to die because to you, they killed your father, and their own daughter."

"Did you want Josie to die?" I asked suddenly, referring to his ex-girlfriend whom he'd stabbed to keep me safe.

"No," he answered honestly, "but I knew her. She never would have stopped, and if we let her go, she would still be trying to either use you, or kill you if she couldn't."

"I think that's the difference," I stated numbly.

Chase pulled away slightly so he could look at me. "What is?"

I shrugged and looked down. "You killed her because it needed to be done, but you would have let her live if there was any other way. You would have let her live even though she tried to kill Jason, and wanted to force me to make portals for the highest bidder."

"I'm . . . sorry?" he said like it was a question.

I shook my head. "That's it exactly. You're *sorry*. You regret her death. I don't. I don't even regret my grandmother's death, even though it was an accident."

"Don't be sorry for being strong, Xoe," he sighed.

"I'm not sorry," I argued, "and that worries me."

Chase leaned his face close to mine, and I thought that he might kiss me when he said, "I'm grateful for who you are, and I know your friends are too. You're loyal and you're just, and regrets have never done anyone any good."

He did kiss me then. The thoughts bouncing around in my head quieted and I just sank into the kiss, reveling in the fact that though it was a relatively new feeling, it was comfortable. I reached my hands up to run them through his hair, wrapping my fingers around the soft tendrils.

Then the front door opened.

My mom stared at us with her jaw agape as we hopped away from each other like magnets with the same polarity. Her newly cut, short, curly brown hair blew about in the breeze as she stood frozen in the doorway, then a small, knowing smile graced her lips.

Before she could say anything, I jumped to my feet. "We're late to meet our friends for pizza," I announced quickly.

My mom continued to smile as she walked over the threshold, removing her lightweight, beige coat. "Okay Xoe," she replied, humoring me. She turned her gaze to Chase. "It's nice to see you again, Chase. It's been too long." Then she *winked* at him and walked into the kitchen.

Feeling like my face was on fire, I shoved Chase toward the front door, pausing only to grab the satchel containing my house keys and wallet on the way out.

Chase turned to face me with a huge grin as I followed him out onto the porch.

I glared playfully at him. "Leave it to you to turn a deep conversation about death and morality into a debacle."

He waggled his eyebrows at me. "Was it at least a *good* debacle?"

I continued to glare. "I wouldn't want to inflate your ego with reassurances."

He laughed and took the hand I offered him. "So do you just plan on popping up right in the middle of Irvine's?"

My glare melted away. I had actually been planning on popping into the parking lot without thinking of the consequences. My traveling power was so new to me, I was yet to consider what might happen if anyone saw me using it.

Chase's expression turned serious. "You weren't *really* going to pop us into the middle of the restaurant, were you?"

I cringed. "Parking lot, actually."

Chase mimicked my cringe. "Think you could navigate to the back parking lot, or maybe an alleyway?"

I had never been to the back lot of Irvine's, so I couldn't bring us there, but I *had* been somewhere else that was relatively private.

I sighed and mumbled, "I really need a car." Then, with a quick look around to make sure no one was watching, we poofed away.

We ended up crammed together in a bathroom stall.

Chase gave me an exasperated look as we stood face to face, only inches away from each other. "Really, Xoe?" he whispered.

I shrugged uncomfortably. "It was the only relatively private place I could think of."

I crouched down in the narrow space to survey the floor for other feet. When none could be found, I opened the stall door and we walked out into the main part of the public restroom.

"And how are we going to explain walking out of the women's bathroom together?" Chase grumbled.

"Just act natural," I instructed as I pushed the door open.

The place was packed since school had let out less than an hour before, but no one seemed to notice as we exited the bathroom. Well, no one but Lucy, who turned to us with wide eyes the moment we appeared. She sat at a table sandwiched by Max and Lela. The three of them wore winter clothes, with their coats draped over the backs of their chairs. Chase and I hadn't thought to grab coats, since we were only outside for a few seconds. So much for keeping up appearances. Normally at that time of year we wouldn't need coats at all, but it had been cold outside with frequent storms.

I scanned the restaurant for Jason and the other wolves, then let out a sigh of relief. They weren't here yet. Feeling light on my feet, I approached Lucy's table with Chase following behind.

Noticing us, Max bobbed his sandy-haired head in acknowledgment. "Where did you guys come from? I was watching the door for you."

"*Yeah*," Lucy said, raising her dark eyebrows almost high enough to meet her hairline. "I'd like to know the same thing."

I slid into the seat across from Lucy. "I couldn't exactly pop into the parking lot, now could I?" I whispered.

Lucy's glare was interrupted as Jason, Emma, and Siobhan entered the restaurant. Seeing us, Jason guided his two charges over to our table. He introduced each of us, including Chase, ending with an, "and you already know Xoe."

Chase took the seat to my right and Jason sat next to him on the end, while Emma took the seat to my left, leaving Siobhan to the other end. The waiter, a boy I thought I recognized from gym class, came and took everyone's drink and pizza orders, then hurried away to the next table.

The conversation initially turned to school, with Lucy assuring Emma that she would help her get caught up. Emma seemed much more comfortable here than she had at my house, perhaps reassured by the presence of two other teenage werewolves. To anyone watching, we would seem like a group of normal teenagers, with Siobhan as our chaperone. Lela was older than us, but looked young enough to pass for someone our age, especially with her messy dark hair, and clothes purchased in the junior's section.

I nodded along with what Lucy was saying, and did my best to avoid eye contact with Chase and Jason. Both of them kept mostly quiet while Lucy dominated the conversation. Needing an uncomplicated target for my eyes, I ended up looking at Siobhan, who was giving Lela a rather unpleasant look. Lela kept her dark eyes steadily on the table.

“Is there a problem?” I asked bluntly, drawing Siobhan's attention to me.

Her green eyes bore into me, and I wondered how I had ever thought that they seemed kind. “Not at all,” she replied evenly, tucking a loose strand of her red hair behind her ear.

Lela dipped her head a little further forward so that her dense, wavy brown hair shielded most of her face.

“Isn't there some rule about lying to your pack leader?” I pressed.

Lela was practically cowering, and if Siobhan was going to be a bully, I wanted to know. Never mind that I had been guilty of bullying Lela in the past. I wasn't about to let someone else do it.

Siobhan just stared at me, but didn't answer my question. I glanced at Lela, but she wouldn't meet my eyes. The rest of the table had gone silent at the exchange.

I looked to my left at Emma. “Is there a reason she's just staring at me?”

Emma cleared her throat and shifted in her seat. "She doesn't see you as dominant to her."

"But I'm her pack leader," I countered, feeling weird talking about Siobhan as if she weren't sitting a few feet away with a cold stare on her face. "She seemed just fine with that this morning."

"That was when Abel was around," Emma explained quickly, then looked down at the table.

I looked back to Siobhan. "Look *lady*," I began, trying to keep my anger in check and failing, "I have been through a lot, and I mean *a lot*, of crap these past few months, and I'm not about to take any more. If you don't want to be here, then *leave*. Otherwise suck it up and stop acting like a spoiled little child who doesn't want to do what the teacher says."

A smile quirked at the corner of Siobhan's lips. "Maybe you're cut out to be Alpha after all," she said, sounding bemused.

I narrowed my eyes at her. "So you were testing me?"

She half-shrugged in reply.

I clenched my teeth in irritation. "Do it again and I'll send you packing back to wherever you came from with third degree burns."

The fine lines around Siobhan's eyes crinkled up as she chuckled. "Yes ma'm," she replied in her southern drawl.

I looked to Lucy and Max, who both shrugged. I

had a sneaking suspicion that Siobhan was going to be a problem, but we'd just have to wait and see.

"Was there anything else you wanted to talk about, Xoe?" Lucy asked, drawing attention away from the small altercation.

I shrugged. I was cranky and ready for Siobhan and Emma to leave so I could update Lucy and Max about my possible haunting situation, and my possible upcoming meeting with Ben and Cynthia. If Siobhan and Emma were going to be part of my pack, I really should have trusted them with the information . . . but I just couldn't bring myself to do it. My trust had been broken one too many times.

"I think we should have occasional meetings," Lucy announced. "Especially once more people start coming in. Just to keep track of everyone and make sure that they're all doing okay."

I shrugged again. "Fine."

Our pizzas arrived. I hadn't finished my turkey sandwich earlier, yet I still found myself without an appetite. Too many adrenaline spikes in one day will do that to you.

I waited impatiently while everyone ate, listening half-heartedly to their chit chat. Max and Jason were catching up, since they hadn't seen each other in a while, leaving Lucy to engage Emma and Siobhan.

I cast a quick glance over at Chase, who gave me a tight-lipped smile. I could tell his impatience matched mine. We both wanted to get on with the show to solve our more pressing problem. Was I being haunted, and if so, what could I do about it?

In an attempt to lighten the mood, I stuck my tongue out at him, then grabbed a piece of pizza despite my queasy stomach.

When the pizza was mostly gone, and the conversation had ebbed, Siobhan announced that she and Emma should get home, as Emma needed to prepare for her first day of school. With a promise from Lucy to meet Emma by the front doors of Shelby High, my new pack members headed out, and Jason stood to follow.

I caught Jason's eye before he could leave. I wanted to tell him what Dorrie had speculated about my grandmother, but I didn't know how to do it, short of making Siobhan and Emma wait outside.

Sensing my predicament he mouthed *later*, then followed the two women out of the building and into the slowly darkening parking lot.

Lela stood next. "I have to work at six in the morning," she announced. "Do you mind if I go too?"

I did mind. I wanted to know what was going on with Siobhan, but given everything else that was happening, it could wait. I nodded my assent and Lela said her goodbyes, then excused herself.

"Okay," I breathed to calm myself. At Max and Lucy's questioning glances, I explained, "I think I'm being haunted by my grandmother."

Max dropped what had been his fifth or sixth slice

of pizza back to his plate and widened his pale green eyes in surprise. "Seriously?"

"She tried to drown her in the kitchen sink," Chase added for me.

Max smirked. "I thought you smelled a little . . . funky."

Lucy punched Max in the shoulder, then turned to me. "How do you know it was your grandmother?"

I shrugged. "It's only speculation. Something hit me in the back shortly after she died, and Dorrie thinks she might have hitched a ride back from the dream realm with us."

"But it could have been any ghost," Lucy argued. "Why do you think it was your grandmother?"

I sighed. "Because that would explain the ghost's motive for trying to drown me, and why it had enough power to almost succeed."

Lucy's almond shaped eyes squinted in thought, then widened suddenly. "You don't know for sure that it was your grandmother. It could have been Bart or Josie."

I inhaled sharply at the idea. It *could* have been either of them. In fact, my grandmother had killed Bartimus in the human world. I wasn't sure on the mechanics of spirits traveling to different planes, but his spirit would have already been in this one. I resisted the urge to look at Chase as I considered Josie. She had been low on the power spectrum, so I highly doubted it was her.

"But why would they just attack now?" I countered. "It's been months since they died."

"It's been nearly two months since your grandmother died," Lucy argued. "If she came back with you from the dreamworld, why did she wait until just now to act?"

I shook my head. "Well hopefully Ben and Cynthia can help us figure it out tonight."

Max, who had picked up his piece of pizza, dropped it again. "Now witches are involved?" he asked incredulously.

"I think so," I replied as I stared down at my own partially eaten slice of pizza. "I received an anonymous text that claimed I had offered my help. Rose, Ben and Cynthia's still-living daughter, is the only person I can recall making that offer to."

"So now we'll be involved with tracking down a murderous demon as well?" Max groaned.

I sighed. "*I* will be involved. As far as I'm concerned, this is demon business. I'm just telling you guys so you know what's going on, and because I need to ask you to keep an eye on Emma and Siobhan while I deal with this."

"Are you sure you don't at least want us to go with you to meet the witches?" Lucy pressed, worry clear in her tone.

I shook my head. "Honestly I'm not worried about it. Without my grandmother or Sam to conspire with, three witches don't pose much of a threat, especially when I can just poof out of there."

Lucy sighed. "What time are you supposed to meet with them?"

"They didn't say. Chase and I will go there after we're done here."

"Well . . . I have homework, so . . . " Lucy trailed off.

"So we're done?" I questioned.

Her face scrunched into apologetic lines. "Sorry."

I smiled. "It's fine. I'd like to get this over with as soon as possible anyway."

Lucy smiled in return as she and Max stood. "Let us know how it goes?" she asked.

I nodded, feeling a little strange at my friends' lack of worry. I couldn't blame them, I did tend to go from one emergency to the next, and I always came out okay. Others got hurt, but not me. I was beginning to feel like I was charmed in a really bad way. Like the universe was saying, "Oh hey, let's help this girl escape mortal peril repeatedly, but as payment we'll kill and maim everyone she cares about."

I didn't know if it was fate, karma, or bittersweet luck, but whatever it was, it was being a real . . . *witch.*

4

Apartment #201 seemed normal enough, except for the itchy feeling I got when I stood too close to the front door. Chase gave me a worried look as he rubbed at the goosebumps that had erupted across his bare arms.

"It feels just like Sasha's house," he commented, referring to the coven's now-deceased head witch.

Sasha had claimed that her home was warded against evil, or to be more specific, *demons*. It hadn't kept me out, but I wasn't a full demon. I shook my head in irritation. "Witches and their wardings."

I reached my hand out to knock, but Chase placed his fingers gently on my wrist. "You sure about this?"

"Nope," I answered, then lifted my hand again to knock anyway.

I heard footsteps approach the door, then there was a pause as someone presumably looked through the peephole. Eventually the door swung inward to reveal Cynthia, looking skinnier than ever with deep purple bags beneath her pale eyes. Her mousy brown hair hung lank around a face riddled with worried lines.

"I didn't think you'd come," she said softly as she stepped aside for Chase and I to enter.

"I almost didn't," I answered honestly. No need to divulge that a big part of the reason I'd chosen to come was because I needed their help.

I looked around at the barren, dark apartment as Cynthia closed and locked the door behind us. The threadbare couch and cheap, wooden furniture led me to believe that the apartment came pre-furnished. Perfect for someone who might need to leave quickly.

"Where's Ben?" I asked, realizing we were the only ones in the apartment.

"He's dead," Cynthia admitted, drawing my gaze back to her. "It's why I contacted you. We'd thought that maybe the demon had left town after killing Sasha, but we were wrong."

I thought of Ben with his tall, skinny frame, glasses, and messy hair. I hadn't particularly liked him, but I still felt a twinge of guilt knowing I probably could have saved him had I decided to pursue the demon earlier.

Cynthia's expression said that she blamed me too, which wasn't fair. They got themselves involved with demons all on their own. So what if my grandmother had manipulated the situation?

"What do you want from me?" I asked, more in answer to her accusing glare than her words.

At my tone, Chase gripped my hand and squeezed, reminding me not to lose my temper.

Cynthia inhaled and let out a shaky breath. "I just want to keep Rose safe."

I squeezed Chase's hand, then let it fall away so I could stand on my own. "And where is Rose?"

The door adjacent to the front door opened to reveal a small closet with Rose inside. "I'm here," she said as she stepped forward, pushing her red bangs out of her eyes. She wore a pale blue sweater set with a knee-length skirt. The clothes looked wildly out of place on her, especially with her blunt-cut red hair. I had a feeling Cynthia was strict on the dress code.

"I told you to stay in there," Cynthia whispered harshly as her daughter came to stand beside her.

Rose rolled her eyes. "I don't think Xoe is the demon we have to fear."

Rose looked healthy and in a much better state than her mom, even though she had lost her father. The thought made me uncomfortable. I had been a total wreck after my dad died.

"Sorry about your father," I said in acknowledgment of Rose sticking up for me.

She shrugged her bony, pre-teen shoulders. "He was only my step-dad."

"Oh," I replied, not knowing what else to say. I hadn't known that information previously. Ben had referred to Claire and Rose as his *daughters*, and though I knew that many step-parents took on the parenting role splendidly, Rose's tone made me think that Ben hadn't been one of them.

I met Rose's defiant gaze, and felt that I couldn't really relate. My teenage years felt so far behind me, even though I was still technically a teenager. Part of me felt like I'd stepped into adult life the day I found out I was a demon.

I walked over to the ugly couch and sat down uninvited, then stared over at Cynthia, letting her know that it was time to get down to business regardless of how we all felt about each other. Chase sat down beside me on the middle seat of the couch, then Rose plonked herself down beside him.

Cynthia's eyes widened at her daughter's behavior, but then she took a chair from the small dining room set, placed it in front of us, and sat.

"I can track the demon," Cynthia began before I could say anything. "I've been tracking it ever since Ben was killed so that I would know if it was coming for us."

"Well then what do you need me for?" I asked sweetly, knowing just what she wanted me for. The wardings in the house were making my nerves twitch, but I did my best to hide it.

"To kill it," she said like it was obvious.

I crossed my arms and leaned back against the couch cushion. I could feel the tension radiating from

Chase. I gave him a small smile, then turned back to Cynthia.

"What's in it for me?"

Cynthia opened her mouth to reply, then closed it as she thought about her answer. "I assumed as a demon, you would want to remedy the situation."

I snorted. "I'm not the demon police. I have no obligation to fix this. So I ask again, what's in it for me?"

Cynthia turned to Chase with a pleading look, obviously hoping that a man would be more compassionate toward her plight.

"I am also not the demon police," he replied when it became clear that Cynthia wasn't going to look away until he said something. "Maybe you should call them."

Cynthia looked back and forth between us, finally letting her desperation leak out into the room. Eventually her eyes settled on me. "What do you want?"

I hadn't come in knowing the exact answer to that question, but what Cynthia had said gave me an idea. "You said you can track this demon, which I assume means you can track any demon. I want you to find the demon that my grandmother was working with, and I want you to summon him fully into this world."

"I-I can't," Cynthia stammered. "Summon him fully, I mean. I'd need a full coven, and something powerful to draw upon. The only demon I've been a part of bringing over was the one who is now after us.

You're grandmother found another way for you and your father, since the first attempt weakened her a great deal. I would need a large amount of demon . . . interference, to even attempt such a thing on my own."

Something akin to hope clenched my stomach into a knot. My dad and I had been carried to the human world by Sam's ghosts, but Cynthia had just confirmed that it was possible to summon a demon fully without that extra factor. "I'm a demon. What if I . . . interfere?"

"I suppose," she said softly, "We could try, at the very least . . . "

I nodded. "Then we'll try. Now I need you to tell me everything you know about the demon that's after you, and where I might find him."

"Can I talk to you in private, Xoe?" Chase interrupted before Cynthia could answer.

I didn't want to talk in private, because I knew what he was going to say, but I nodded and stood. We both walked out of the apartment to stand in the fading sunlight of the stairwell, shutting the front door behind us.

"I don't think this is a good idea," Chase stated as he glanced out at the mostly empty parking lot. "Working with witches to summon Sam . . . what if another demon comes through?"

"Do you have any better suggestions?" I countered.

Chase took a deep breath and let it out. "Why don't we have Cynthia try to contact whomever is haunting you? You know, go directly to the source."

I quirked an eyebrow at him. "Do you really think only two witches summoning what is probably a rather powerful ghost is a good idea? Sam seems to have control over his spirits. It just seems safer."

Chase smiled bitterly. "You're right. I know you are. I just didn't want to have to ask Sam for a favor once we found him."

"What were you planning on doing if you found him before this all happened?"

Chase shrugged and wouldn't quite meet my eyes.

"Well?" I pressed.

He shrugged again. "I guess I would have given him a good pummeling until he told me what your dad was looking into before he died, then I would have told him to keep running so that you wouldn't kill him."

My jaw dropped in surprise. "I wouldn't have killed him!" I whispered harshly.

Chase looked at me like I was being silly, and I frowned back at him. "I wouldn't kill your *brother*, no matter how badly I wanted to."

"You nearly killed him the last time we saw him . . . " Chase accused softly.

I suddenly felt cold, and it wasn't from the chilly breeze. I *had* been ready to kill Sam after my father died. It was not a good memory.

"We should get back inside," I murmured.

"Xoe-" Chase began, but I held up a hand to cut him off.

Without another word I re-entered the apartment.

Rose and Cynthia were still in their seats, so I resumed mine. Chase came in a moment later and shut the door behind him. He retook his seat, looking at me like he really wanted to say something, but he kept his mouth shut.

"So tell me about this demon," I prompted again once we were all settled.

Cynthia's eyes took on a faraway look, and I realized that I was asking her to describe the killer of not only her husband, but her daughter.

"She looks to be around your age, maybe a few years older," Cynthia explained as she met my eyes. "Shoulder-length dark hair, small frame, a few inches shorter than you," she went on.

For some reason I had envisioned a demon more like Bartimus. I had *not* envisioned a young demon girl like . . . well, like me.

"Usually, when I track her I only get glimpses," Cynthia continued. "I can tell whether she's close or far, and I can get a general idea of where she is, but not exactly."

So in other words, you're not as helpful as you led us to believe, I thought. What I said out loud was, "Were you there when, you know, with Ben?"

Moisture became apparent around Cynthia's eyes. She tried to open them wide enough that tears wouldn't fall, but was unsuccessful. She looked down at her lap as she wiped her tears, embarrassed, though there was no need to be. There was nothing wrong with crying.

"She was there," Rose answered for her. "They had been tracking the demon from the beginning. She had disappeared for a long time, so that's why we stayed in Shelby. We thought it would be the last place she would look if she believed we were on the run. Then she popped up again and my parents went to investigate."

"So the demon might not have been after Ben?" I questioned.

"W-what do you mean?" Cynthia cut in, raising her tear-stained face to look at me.

I did my very best not to roll my eyes, but it was a struggle. "Two witches confront an unsuspecting demon who was thrown into the human world against her will without a home or anyone that she knows. It's a recipe for disaster, no matter the demon's intentions."

"But she killed Claire and Sasha," Cynthia countered sharply. "She obviously has a vendetta."

I shrugged. "As far as I've been told, their bodies were found well-after the altercations took place. No one really knows what happened, or why the demon attacked."

Cynthia's expression turned hostile. "Are you implying that my daughter somehow provoked this demon?"

I shook my head. "Not at all, though I wouldn't put it past Sasha. All I'm saying is that we have no idea *why* the demon killed just Claire and Sasha, or what the circumstances were that led to their deaths."

Cynthia began crying again. "We know that the demon brutally murdered them. That should be enough." She sniffled and met my eyes, daring me to argue.

I shrugged. "I guess we'll just have to find out once we meet her."

"Kill her, you mean."

I took a deep breath and thought about Cynthia's innocent daughter Claire, found torn to shreds in her bed. Ben, I didn't care about. He got what you get for playing with demons. Claire hadn't done anything wrong, at least as far as I knew.

"Yes. That's what I mean."

Cynthia breathed a sigh of relief. "When would you like to try summoning this other demon?"

"One would think you'd be a little more hesitant about summoning another demon," I accused.

Cynthia looked like she tasted something sour. Her tears had stopped to once again be replaced by anger. "*Trust me*, when all of this is over, I will gladly go back to pretending demons don't exist, but I can't do that with this girl gunning for our deaths."

I replied with a curt nod, satisfied with her answer. "What will you need from me?"

Cynthia shrugged. "Power . . . energy? It's best if you're well rested before we try. It might take a lot out of you."

"Well that rules out tonight," I groaned. At Rose and Cynthia's questioning glances I clarified, "It's been a *very* long day."

"Then let's plan on tomorrow," Cynthia replied, "and if I get a sense of where the demon girl is before then, I'll call."

"Nice and simple," I replied.

Cynthia nodded. Rose and Chase nodded. We were all in agreement, nice and simple. Nice, like how hungry crocodiles are nice, and simple, akin to quantum physics.

5

By the time Chase and I poofed back into my bedroom at my mom's house, I was exhausted. Of course Chase, being a night owl, and not having had a rough morning like mine, was bright-eyed and bushy tailed.

"Do you want me to take you back underground?" I asked with a yawn as we each took a seat on my bed.

Chase smiled at me and shook his head. "I'm not about to let you get suffocated by a pillow in your sleep."

I sighed, he was probably right. My mom wouldn't allow a boy to sleep in my room, but judging by the lack of sound in the rest of the house, she was already asleep. What she didn't know wouldn't hurt her. The thought was actually kind of exciting. Not the Chase staying in my room part, that just made me nervous, but the teenage act of sneaking a boy into my room.

Maybe I wasn't a forty year-old trapped in a seventeen year-old's body after all.

With a nod to Chase I stood and began rifling through my dresser for any pajamas that weren't horribly unbecoming, then I excused myself to the adjoining bathroom to change.

Before I could take off my jeans, my cell phone buzzed in my pocket. I took it out to see a text from Jason, and suddenly remembered him mouthing *"later"*. Apparently it was now *later.*

Half dressed, I opened the text which read, "What did you find out about your kitchen experience?"

I dropped my flannel pajama bottoms to the floor to reply, "Being haunted. Probably by my grandmother."

The phone buzzed a moment later with, "What?!?!"

I smiled. "Tomorrow Cynthia will try to 'contact' Sam. He could help if we can find him."

I waited a full minute for a reply, but when it didn't happen I began dressing again. Just as I was about to wash my face, the phone buzzed from its perch on the side of my bathtub.

The new message read, " . . . well I'm glad you have it all figured out."

I frowned. Was he upset that I hadn't involved him in the whole figuring out aspect? Was he upset as a friend, or as an ex-boyfriend? Jason was over one-hundred years old, and it made his motives more difficult to comprehend than those of other boys. He'd already lived a full life-time or two, while I was sitting here floundering over my first breakup.

Not having a clue how to handle this whole awkward situation, I typed, "I'd ask you to come, but you have to watch Emma . . . "

" . . . Yeah." he replied. "Just be careful, Okay?"

I nodded, then realizing there was no way for him to see it, I typed, "Careful is my middle name."

"More like Calamitous," he replied instantly.

I laughed quietly. "GOODNIGHT Jason," I typed.

"Goodnight Calamity Xoe," he messaged back.

I put my phone down and continued getting ready for bed, while I debated on where I'd make Chase sleep. Two months ago I would have had him sleep in my bed. He was one of my best friends, and we had fallen asleep watching movies next to each other plenty of times at my dad's house. It was always comfortable. Now suddenly it made me nervous. Could a kiss or two really change that much?

I took a deep breath. Why should I let a kiss change everything? He had slept next to me before, and it would be just plain weird to make him sleep on the floor now.

With things settled in my mind, I exited the bathroom, only to find Chase rolling out the sleeping bag that usually stayed in my closet.

"What are you doing?" I asked as he stood.

"I just wasn't sure . . . " he trailed off.

"We've slept in the same bed plenty of times," I

said, like I hadn't just been wracking my brain over the same dilemma.

"I just didn't want to *presume*," he replied, drawing out the word "presume".

I rolled my eyes at him. "I left an extra toothbrush by the sink."

Chase nodded and began humming softly as he went into the bathroom. I knew humming was his nervous tick, but he didn't know that I'd drawn that conclusion. The notes were almost too soft to hear, but it sounded like *Somewhere Over the Rainbow*.

While he prepared for bed, I returned the sleeping bag to my closet, plugged my phone in to charge, and crawled into bed. At first I scooted myself all the way against the wall, then told myself to stop being silly and took on a more comfortable position on one side of the bed.

Moments later Chase emerged from the bathroom, slipped off his shoes, and climbed into bed still wearing his tee shirt and jeans, since he didn't have any pajamas. I would have offered him some of my baggy ones, but with his height they'd still probably be too small.

He laid on his back while I laid on my side facing him.

"You want to get the light?" I asked softly.

Without a word, he reached over and switched off the bedside lamp, leaving us bathed in the sparse moonlight shining through my bedroom window.

"Hey Xoe?" he asked softly.

"Hmm?" I mumbled.

"Let the witches draw from me when we summon Sam."

I smiled in the darkness. "Nope."

I felt the bed shift slightly as Chase sighed. "I had to try."

I scooted over and laid my head on his shoulder. He tensed for a moment, then slipped his arm underneath me to wrap around my back and pull me a little closer. I relaxed, not allowing myself to think about the implications of a late-night snuggle. All I could think about was how I missed the time I'd spent living in my dad's house with him and Chase. I missed the three of us having morning coffee together, and I missed watching old *Seinfeld* reruns in my dad's den. Chase and I would often fall asleep on the couch, while my dad passed out in the adjacent recliner. It had made me feel *safe*.

Yet, I'd spent that whole time wallowing about dropping out of high school, and about not being able to find Jason. I regretted not appreciating that time with my dad while I still had it.

I felt Chase's body relax into sleep, but I suddenly felt very awake. Chase had known my dad longer than I had, and I knew that he missed him too, though he didn't really talk about it. Chase didn't really talk about much, not about his past, or his sadness, or even his fond memories that most people would be comfortable sharing.

I flashed back on a memory of the three of us in the kitchen. My dad had wanted me to try re-heating the cup of coffee in his hand with my powers. I had ended up boiling it with such ferocity that it shot out of his cup and drenched his entire arm. Luckily like me, he was unable to get burned by hot liquids, or anything else for that matter. We'd all laughed, and it had become an ongoing joke any time I was near a cup of coffee.

I smiled at the memory even though it made my heart hurt. Fighting back tears, I snuggled a little closer to Chase, wishing we were going to sleep at my dad's house, even if he wasn't there.

Either I woke Chase up, or he sensed my discomfort from a stage of half-sleep, but his hand began to gently rub circles along my back in a comforting gesture. I did cry then, just a few tears, as I let out a silent wish for things to go back to how they had been, just two months before.

I KNEW I WAS DREAMING, since logically I knew that I was lying in my bed in the human world, but standing in the middle of my dad's kitchen with him brewing us a fresh pot of coffee felt so real that it hurt.

As the coffee maker dripped its last drop, my dad filled up two mugs and handed one to me.

"She won't give up," he said conversationally as his blond hair fell forward to cover one of his green eyes.

"Grandma?" I asked.

My dad nodded.

"How is she even doing this?" I asked as I sipped my dream coffee. "She's *dead*."

He shrugged. "She has some sort of hold on you, though I don't understand it. It's given her a great deal of power."

"Then how are *you* here?" I pressed. "Do you have some sort of hold on me as well?"

He chuckled. "This is a dream, Alexondra. I'm *not* here."

"But-" I began

He cut me off with a nervous glance to the side, as if hearing something I couldn't. He held a finger up to his lips for me to be quiet while he looked around the room. Heart thudding in my chest, I stayed perfectly still and listened for whatever he sensed.

"You have to go now," he said quickly.

"But-" I argued again, but he took hold of my shoulders and shoved me.

If it had been a real shove, I would have fallen down. Instead I woke with a gasp and sat up in bed. Chase sat up with me and placed a hand on my back while I tried to catch my breath.

"What happened?" he asked frantically. "Did she attack you again?"

I shook my head and held a hand to my chest. My

heart was beating a million miles per minute. "My dad," I breathed.

Chase's eyes widened.

I took a deep, shuddering breath. "It was just a dream," I rasped.

Chase put a hand on my shoulder and waited for me to meet his eyes. "We both know that your dreams aren't *just* dreams."

He was right. I had a knack for premonitory dreams, but this one felt different. It had felt like my dad was really there.

I shook my head while my breathing and heart rate slowed. "Nothing has changed. We'll still summon Sam tonight and we'll get rid of grandmother dearest once and for all."

Chase watched me for a moment, framed by the square of morning light coming in through the window, then nodded and climbed out of bed. "We should check on Dorrie this morning," he announced, changing the subject. "Plus, I wouldn't mind a change of clothes."

I nodded in reply, grateful for the subject change. "I should say hi to my mom first. I haven't seen her since-"

"You kissed me," he finished.

I glared at him from my perch on the bed. "Since *you* kissed *me*."

He offered me a crooked smile. "That's not how I remember it."

I scrunched my nose at him, then climbed out of bed. I could hear coffee being ground downstairs, and hoped it was just my mom making a second pot; half for me, and half for her to take in her thermos to work. If it was the first pot, she'd have plenty of time to hang around giving me a hard time about kissing Chase.

I left Chase in my room and went downstairs, still wearing my pajamas. I reached the kitchen to find my mom already dressed in a green button up shirt and black slacks. Second pot. Goody.

Silently cheering in my head, I gave the kitchen sink a wary glance as I approached my mom. Seeing me, she pulled out my favorite *Edgar Allen Poe* mug and poured me a fresh cup of coffee. The smell of my favorite liquid brought my dream rushing back to me, but I brushed it off as my mom eyed me expectantly.

I held up my hand to shield my face from the harsh morning like streaming in through the kitchen window while I stared back at her. "*What?*"

"So Chase, huh?" she asked as she pushed her short, wavy hair away from her face.

I lifted my nose in the air. "I don't know what you're talking about."

My mom smiled, then turned to pop a bagel into the toaster. "You two dating now?"

I grimaced. "I'm not dating *anyone*."

She gave me a scrutinizing look over her shoulder with her dark brown eyes. "That's not what it looked like to me . . . "

I sighed. I hadn't even spoken about it with my friends yet. I sure as heck didn't want to discuss it with my mother. "It just *happened*."

"Is that why he's in your bedroom right now?" she asked casually.

I inhaled my coffee in surprise, then went into a fit of sputtering as I tried to clear my airways, all while sloshing coffee all over my hand and onto the floor.

"Come again?" I managed to choke out.

She raised an eyebrow as she pulled the bagel out of the toaster and began to spread cream cheese on it. "You didn't lock your door. I peeked inside your room this morning to make sure you had made it home last night."

I grabbed a kitchen rag and began to clean up my spilled coffee. "And you didn't kick him out?" I asked weakly as I kneeled on the floor.

My mom sighed. "I know the two of you lived in your dad's house together. I think I'm just relieved to have you both here, instead of down there."

I stood and tossed the wet rag into the empty sink. "Is this a trick?" I asked suspiciously.

"I also noted that both of you had clothes on. If you plan for that to change at any point, I expect you to talk to me about it first."

"Mom!" I exclaimed, feeling like my face was on fire. I was also very glad at that moment that Chase was up in my room where he hopefully couldn't hear us.

She gave me her best *mom* look as she said, "I mean it, Xoe."

I really wanted to run away to my room, but what I said was, "Don't expect *that* talk to come any time soon."

My mom put the cream-cheesed bagel on a plate and handed it to me. "Tell your *boyfriend* to come down for coffee. I can be a few minutes late for work."

I opened my mouth as I tried to think of something to say. "Um, we really need to go check on my friend in the underground."

My mom raised an eyebrow at me. "If you're going to have boys staying in your room in *my* house, the least the both of you can do is have coffee with me."

Sighing, I nodded and left the kitchen to march dutifully upstairs, bagel and coffee in hand. This at least wasn't as bad as the time Max and Jason had both slept on the floor of my room. Now *that* would have made for an awkward coffee session. Of course, I hadn't even kissed Jason at that point, and I had no intention of *ever* kissing Max, even if he wasn't dating Allison.

I entered my room to find Chase leafing through a world atlas from my bookshelf. "You know," he began as I closed the door behind me, "it's a shame you can only appear in places you've been, or else we could be in Japan right now."

I snorted. "Mom wants you to come down for coffee."

Chase dropped the atlas to his lap and looked at me in shock. "... What?"

I smirked and waved a hand for him to follow me. "C'mon."

What ensued when we went back downstairs was ten times more frightening than my evil grandmother's ghost. Okay, maybe frightening isn't the word. We'll go with awkward. *Extremely* awkward.

It started with my mom telling us we were *allowed* to sit next to each other (we had taken seats as far apart as possible), and ended with her asking Chase about his previous relationships. That question had really thrown us, considering we'd *killed* Chase's last girlfriend.

When she finally had to go to work, I was able to shower, and we popped underground for me to hang out with Dorrie while Chase showered.

My tension melted as soon as I sat down in my dad's den, even if it was to play another game of Checkers with Dorrie. We ended up staying there most of the day since Lucy, Allison, Emma, and Max were in school. Dorrie was thrilled. If she had her way, we would have stayed the night, but I explained to her that I needed to check in with Lucy to make sure Emma's first day went okay, and I needed to check in with Jason to make sure there was still no sign of Emma's father, though he probably would have called me if there was.

Dorrie watched us sadly as Chase and I both joined hands to leave the underground. The look on her face before we poofed out of existence let me know that we'd need to figure out something other than leaving her trapped in my dad's house all of the time. The only problem was that I didn't see any other options. She no longer had a cab to drive in the dreamworld, and if she went out into the demon world, she would be *unmade*.

Drivers weren't allowed to leave the dreamworld. They weren't even allowed to leave their cabs. Personally, I thought that Dorrie at least had a better life now than when I'd first met her, but I wasn't the one that could never leave the house, with only Chase and myself for company.

Maybe I could bring her to my mom's house and my friends could come over and visit with her. It would be risky, but not as risky as bringing a group of non-demons to the underground again. Plus, Dorrie might enjoy having her boundaries expanded, if only a little.

I continued thinking about Dorrie as we appeared in my empty living room, then left to walk to Lucy's. Chase and I were both silent, deep in our own thoughts as our feet crunched along the gravel at the edge of the road. The cool wind whipped my loose hair about, while the smell of damp earth pervaded my nostrils. Fresh air was the one thing I really missed when I was in the underground. The demons did their best to magically replicate the outdoors, but that deep, instinctual sense that we all have gave the illusion away.

It would have been nice if the walk to Lucy's was

longer, extending our time outdoors. Plus, it was hard to be excited about what lay at the end of our journey. Checking in on the status of my new pack members seemed like a menial task compared to what we'd be doing later that night. I knew Chase's thoughts were likely on the idea of seeing his brother again, that was, if Cynthia could actually summon him.

I was surprised when Chase reached out and grabbed my hand as we walked. He did so without a word. Sure, I had considered grabbing his hand as well, but I didn't know if we were at that point yet. I had told him that I needed to be on my own for a while, which was true, but it had been over six weeks since Jason and I broke up. Was that long enough? I wasn't sure, but boy, did his hand ever feel nice in mine.

6

I had just raised my hand to knock on Lucy's door when my phone buzzed. I checked it to find a text from Cynthia's number that read, "Found her."

I showed the text to Chase, just as Lucy opened the door. Instantly reading the looks on our faces, Lucy's eyes narrowed. "What's going on?" she asked suspiciously.

"Cynthia just picked up on the demon girl's location," I explained hurriedly.

"Demon . . . girl?" Lucy asked, making me remember that I hadn't talked to her since we'd met with Cynthia and Rose.

"We have to go," I said quickly. "I'll explain later."

"I'm coming," Lucy demanded. Without waiting for an answer, she grabbed her black pea coat from the coat rack beside her front door, then stepped back for us to come inside.

Not wanting to take the time to argue, Chase and I stepped into Lucy's house, shutting the door behind us. I did a quick scan of the beige living room to make sure we were alone, then held my hands out to Chase and Lucy. They each took one. Adrenaline rushing through my veins, I concentrated on Cynthia and Rose's little, dingy apartment.

Rose let out a yip of surprise when we appeared, then a smile slowly crossed her freckled face. "*That* is so cool," she marveled.

I dropped Lucy and Chase's hands, and I rolled my eyes. "Where's your mom?"

"I'm in here!" Cynthia called from the small, adjoining kitchen.

I walked around the narrow divider of counter top, with Lucy and Chase following close behind me, to find Cynthia seated on the kitchen floor. She had a map of Shelby in front of her, covered in what looked like white sand.

She pointed to an area where the sand had gathered on the map without looking up. "She's *there*," she explained, "but there's no telling how long she'll stay."

I looked to where Cynthia pointed. It was an area downtown where tourists and the more *hip* denizens of Shelby liked to hang out, filled with coffee shops, bars, and bookstores.

"How will we find her?" Lucy asked. "There have to

be half a dozen cafes and restaurants in that small area alone. Do we even know what she looks like?"

Cynthia turned startled eyes to us as she finally realized that it wasn't just me and Chase hovering over her. "Can't demons sense their own kind?" she asked, puzzled.

I shook my head at Cynthia, then turned my gaze to Lucy. "Do you think you'd be able to smell her?"

Lucy shrugged. "How much demon blood does she have?"

At the same time, Cynthia and Rose answered, "A lot."

Lucy puckered her dainty, cupid's bow lips in thought. "If we cross an area where she was, I might be able to pick up on a scent. More likely though, we'd have to walk through each establishment so I could get close enough to smell the patrons."

I bit my lip. Those did not seem like good odds. "It's worth a shot," I conceded. I held my hands out to my friends once again, then met Cynthia's eyes as I said, "Call me if she moves."

A moment later we were all standing in an alley way.

Chase looked around at the trash strewn street. "I don't even want to know why you've been *here* before."

I couldn't help my wry smile. "I was kidnapped out of this very alleyway by those witches that wanted to steal my powers."

Chase's eyebrows raised as he realized what I was

talking about, and Lucy just frowned. She had been kidnapped during that fun little experience as well.

"Let's go," I announced, not wanting to dwell on the memory.

We made our way to the main street, which was fairly populated, even for a weekday. We stared at the passersby as the gravity of the task ahead hit us. Finding the demon girl was going to be like finding a needle in a haystack, except this needle had a tendency to brutally murder people.

Chase and Lucy looked to me for instruction. "We should split up," I said in reply to their questioning glances. "You two stick together and check the buildings on this side of the street, and I'll check the other side."

"You shouldn't go alone," Chase said instantly.

I smirked at him. "If worse comes to worse, I can poof away from danger. Neither of you can do that, so you should go together."

"But you can't smell her like I can," Lucy argued, crossing her delicate arms in defiance.

"I know what she looks like," I explained. "If I find someone that fits the description, I'll call you to come smell her. You have your cell on you, right?"

Lucy nodded, obviously unhappy with the situation. Chase's face mirrored hers perfectly.

"Do you guys have any better ideas?" I asked of their petulant expressions.

When they didn't answer, I nodded my head and

left them to walk across the street. I glanced back once I reached the other side to see them entering the nearest coffee shop together, looking like a strange couple since Chase was over a foot taller than Lucy.

I turned and went into the Italian restaurant in front of me, suddenly feeling unsure about my task. The interior of the restaurant was dimly lit, and as far as I could see, the color scheme was dark reds and black. The host, a middle aged man whose belly was a little too large for his tuxedo shirt, waited dutifully to seat any who entered.

He watched me with a disinterested look on his face as I approached. "One?" he asked apathetically.

"I'm meeting someone," I explained. "Mind if I look around to see if she's here?"

He sighed and gave a lazy nod, and I passed by him without another thought. Fortunately the restaurant was small, and most of the patrons were either older couples, or families with young children. It didn't take me long to see that the demon girl was not among the diners, but I decided to do a quick check of the bathroom, just in case.

I walked confidently across the restaurant and opened the door to the women's restroom. The bathroom was in stark contrast to the restaurant, done in sterile whites with water stains on the ceiling and walls. What a hole.

I stepped inside and let the door swing shut behind me, then peeked under the bathroom stalls. Two of the three stalls were empty, but the third revealed black combat boots. Biting my lip in frustration, I turned to a sink and slowly washed my hands in hopes that the mystery girl in the stall would emerge before too long.

As I looked into the cloudy glass mirror above the sink, I thought I saw a flash of movement, but it was gone before I could make out what it was. I leaned sideways to glance underneath the occupied stall. The feet were still there.

I went back to washing my hands, feeling suddenly uneasy. The tiny hairs on the back of my neck prickled as I glanced at the boot-clad feet once again, but they hadn't moved.

The toilet flushed, startling me so that I banged my hands against the faucet as I shoved them back underneath the flow of water. I watched the closed stall door in the mirror while I waited, wondering what the heck was taking the girl so long. Suddenly, something sharp was at my throat and I was pulled backward. Whoever had me spun me around so I couldn't see anything in the bathroom mirrors.

"*Why* are you here?" a feminine voice spat in my ear.

I wiped my wet hands on my jeans and tried to turn my head far enough to see her, but it was no good. The sharp pressure at my throat made speaking highly uncomfortable, but I managed to reply, "To wash my hands, you freak. It is a bathroom after all."

The pressure increased at my throat, and realizing I

had no other choice, I closed my eyes and pictured the far end of the bathroom. Suddenly I was free, and facing the girl Cynthia had described.

My eyes widened in surprise as I took in the white apron over her casual clothes, and the hairnet that held her dark hair away from her face. She clenched her strong, angular jaw in annoyance. Sparing the time to glare at me with her large, hazel eyes, she stomped over to the bathroom door and locked it.

"Who are you?" she asked as she marched back toward me. "I can sense a demon from a mile away." Face to face, I could tell that Cynthia had been correct about the girl's height. She was three, maybe four inches shorter than my 5'8".

"Y-you work here?" I asked, glancing at her hairnet. I was more surprised by that fact than the fact that this rather innocent looking girl had just tried to slit my throat. I didn't see a knife anywhere, but she could have easily stashed it in her apron.

Her eyes narrowed as she looked at me, *actually* looked at me, then her jaw dropped in surprise. "You look just like her," she commented softly.

I sighed. "I imagine you're referring to my grandmother?"

She looked me up and down again. "Shorter. Not as polished, but you could otherwise easily pass as sisters."

Bitterness boiled in my stomach at the thought of my grandmother's face, so similar to mine. More powerful demons didn't age, and my grandmother had been one of the most powerful demons around.

We both turned as someone tried to open the bathroom door. The girl walked over and opened it to peek outside, then told whoever it was that a toilet had overflowed and she was cleaning it up. She shut and locked the door again, then turned back to me.

"What do you want, Alexondra?" she asked coldly.

I raised an eyebrow at her. "You must have actually spent some time around my grandmother if you know my name."

She snorted. "Everyone knows *your* name. Your dad is a well-known demon."

My heart stopped for a moment at the mention of my dad. She had said *is*, letting me know that she didn't know he was dead. Of course, she had been trapped in the human world. How would she know?

"I know about the witches you killed," I commented casually, hoping to catch her off guard.

Rage washed over her face, then suddenly dissipated. "You wouldn't have such a look of judgment on your face if you knew what they did to me. I bet they're playing the victims here."

"Oh?" I prompted, not wanting to give away what I did and didn't know.

"Alexandria had them torture me," she said, her voice firm and even. "She wanted to know what I know, but I escaped. Now they're all going to pay."

Was this girl crazy? "Know what you know?" I asked.

The girl gave me an *as if* look. "Why are you here again?"

"What's your name?" I asked instead, in an attempt to calm her down. She seemed about ready to either run away, or attack me again.

"Nix," she replied without thinking about it. "Now *tell me why you're here*."

"I'm here to bring you back to the underground," I lied.

"Pffft," Nix replied. "I'm not going back until I make the witches pay. *All of them*. I may not be able to get to Alexandria yet, but I'll find a way."

"My grandmother and my dad are both *dead*," I forced myself to say, "and I'm running out of patience."

A look of almost sympathy crossed Nix's face, then she scowled. My phone started buzzing in my pocket. Nix glanced at it, then glanced at the door. Sensing that she was about to run, I lunged for her, hoping to pop her into the underground, where at least she couldn't kill any more witches.

I landed one hand on her arm and was about to transport us out of there when she swatted at me with her free hand. What should have been an ineffective blow landed me with what looked like four knife slices across my forearm.

I released her arm and tried to drop to the floor as she swatted at me again, but I wasn't fast enough.

Sharp pain seared across my stomach, followed by the warmth of fresh blood. Panicking, I chucked a small fireball at her as I skittered backward. She dodged the fire, unlocked the bathroom door, and ran, leaving me to clutch at my wounds in shock. I collapsed the rest of the way to the tile floor as blood slowly soaked through my clothing.

My phone started buzzing again. I scowled, having to straighten out my right leg from my seat on the floor to fish it out of my pocket with my good arm. My eyes widened as I glanced at the floor to see just how much blood I was losing. Nix must have really done a number on me, but it was hard to tell with the chilly sensation creeping through my entire body. I fumbled with my phone as Chase's number flashed in front of my face before I pushed the answer button.

"*Yeah*?" I groaned into the receiver.

"We haven't seen a sign of her . . . but I'm guessing you did?" Chase replied.

"I'm currently bleeding onto the floor, worrying about what diseases I might pick up from this bathroom," I explained, feeling oddly numb.

"Where are you?" he demanded.

"The Italian restaurant across from where we parted," I replied breathily. "Walking out of here in my current state will probably draw way too much attention, so I'll just meet you guys in the alleyway."

"We can come and get you," he offered.

"No," I answered quickly. "Just meet me in the alley. And Chase?"

"Yeah?" he replied.

"If you see this girl between now and then, do *not* approach her."

I could almost sense him nodding on the other end of the line. "If you say so," he replied just before hanging up.

I groaned again as I looked down at my blood-soaked clothing, then pictured the alleyway. I was feeling tired from blood loss, and nothing happened at first. I almost thought I'd have to call Chase back, but then with a final burst of effort, I managed to poof out.

As soon as I re-formed, I collapsed in the dirty alleyway, clutching my arms against my midsection to slow the bleeding.

"Xoe!" I heard Lucy shout. I felt lightheaded and nauseous as I looked up to see her and Chase running toward me.

Chase arrived first, gathered me into his arms, and lifted me up to cradle me in his arms. My eyes were closed, but I could hear Lucy panting, so she was close by.

"We need to get you to a hospital," Chase stated.

"No hospital," I slurred, feeling groggy as I forced my eyes open. "I just need some bandages and rest." I didn't need to explain to a doctor why my knife wounds were healing faster than normal, or why I had knife wounds to begin with. "I don't think I can take us," I added.

Way ahead of me on that point, Lucy already had her phone lifted to her ear. "Allison isn't answering," she stated as she ended the call, then selected another number to dial.

I looked up at Chase woozily as he held me with one arm under my knees and the other under my shoulders. There seemed to be pretty lights dancing around his head, or maybe it was just the sunlight playing tricks on me.

I heard Lucy giving someone directions, then her face appeared above me. "Jason is on his way," she stated.

Of course he was.

7

The next ten minutes were a blur. I remained in Chase's arms while Lucy kept up a constant stream of conversation to keep me awake. I'd had to shut down several more suggestions that we should go to the hospital, and there had probably been a few more that I didn't quite hear. It was getting difficult to focus on Lucy's words, and I felt like I was floating in Chase's arms.

Suddenly Jason was there. I felt his hand on my face, but felt unable to focus as he looked down into my eyes. My eyes fluttered closed as Chase climbed into the backseat of Jason's car with me still in his arms. The sound of car doors shutting echoed distantly, then the car lurched into movement.

Each turn made me want to vomit, and I kept trying to open my eyes, but couldn't seem to manage it.

Lucy's voice melted into my awareness as she asked, "Where are we going?"

Jason was silent, then I heard Chase whisper, "To the hospital."

"But she said no hospital," Lucy replied at full volume.

"There's no other choice," Chase replied, his voice suddenly closer than before. I felt him kiss my temple, then he whispered, "Just stay with me, Xoe."

It was only then that I realized I might be dying.

I OPENED my eyes to a bright light. I'll admit, the thought that I might be dead flashed through my mind, but then I heard the sound of medical equipment in the background, amidst the murmur of muffled voices.

I tried to sit up as the room came into focus, but didn't get far before someone appeared at my side to help me.

"Just relax, sweetie, you're fine."

The sound of my mom's voice helped calm my panic as the events that had led to me being hospitalized came flooding back. I looked down at my arm to see a fresh white bandage covering the wounds, and I could feel another bandage underneath my hospital gown. In my other arm was an IV filled with clear fluid.

"Where are my friends?" I asked weakly, turning my head to look at my mom.

Her face was lined with worry, but she put on a brave smile. "They're waiting outside. Allison and Max are here too, and a gentlemen that's a little too old to be hanging out with you."

I cringed. She had to be talking about either Abel or Devin. "Blond-haired *GQ* model, or tall, dark, and erm, exotic?"

"Blond," she said levelly, still waiting for an explanation.

"He's part of the werewolf coalition," I whispered conspiratorially, feeling slightly loopy. They must have had me on some serious pain meds for them to overpower my demon metabolism.

My mom's eyes widened. Though she knew all about my strange little world, I tried to keep her out of it as much as possible.

"Are you in trouble?" she whispered back.

It took me a moment to realize what she meant, then it occurred to me that she probably thought Devin was there to punish me.

I smiled weakly. "He's just here to make sure I'm okay. Abel, the one who's not here, was friends with dad."

My mom's mouth formed an "o" of understanding, then she asked, "What happened, Xoe?"

I knew the question had been coming, and I had absolutely no answer for it. "I don't remember," I lied.

My mom raised both her eyebrows in disbelief.

"You're in the hospital with eight knife-wounds, and you don't remember what happened?"

I shrugged and felt an uncomfortable tightness in my abdomen. Wondering how many stitches I had, I gave my mom an apologetic look.

"You can tell me, Xoe," she said evenly.

I bit my lip. I *could* tell her, but I couldn't expect her to lie to the hospital staff. "Maybe later," I replied, "but for now, I don't remember."

My mom looked like she wanted to say something else, but there was a knock on the door. A young woman in scrubs opened the door and leaned the top of her body into the room.

"Her friends are asking to see her," the woman announced, speaking to my mom instead of me.

My mom nodded, and gestured for the woman to get them.

"Only three allowed at a time," the woman stated.

My mom sighed in annoyance and stood, then looked down at me. "Who should I send back?"

"The three that brought me here?" I asked hopefully.

She sighed again, then slumped her shoulders in defeat before following the nurse out of the room. A few minutes later the door opened again to reveal Chase, Jason, and Lucy. I was suddenly glad for the light blanket draped over most of my body, since the flimsy hospital gown didn't really offer much cover.

Lucy was the first to reach my side. She gently

grabbed my hand as she crouched beside the hospital bed. Words tumbled out of her mouth. "I was so scared, Xoe. By the time we got here you were unconscious. If I wasn't able to hear your heartbeat, I would have thought you were dead."

I squeezed her hand with what little strength I had, then turned my gaze to the boys. "Thanks," I said, acknowledging both of them with my eyes.

They both looked at each other, then back at me. I could tell they had a lot to say, but neither spoke.

"I didn't get a chance to ask my mom how long I needed to be in here," I stated, hoping that one of them had the answer.

"One more night," Lucy informed me, "and bed rest after that, though with your healing rate, you'll probably be fine by morning."

It was good news, but it still had me feeling nervous. "I really don't want to stay here overnight."

"And we don't think you should," Chase explained as he and Jason each took a few steps closer to hover around me. "The hospital only allows family after 8pm, and with the sink incident, and now this attack, we don't feel like leaving you and your mom alone is a good idea. Plus, like Lucy said, you'll heal much faster than the doctors would expect. You don't need any extra attention."

"So what do we do?" I asked, agreeing with them whole-heartedly.

"We need to convince your mom to sign you out,"

Jason answered, "but she doesn't believe that we don't know what happened, and neither do the cops."

I gulped. "Cops?"

Jason looked down at me sympathetically. "A teenage girl shows up at the hospital with multiple knife wounds . . . " he trailed off.

"The cops will want to ask questions," I finished for him. "I told my mom that I don't remember anything, but she doesn't believe me."

"You should probably tell that to the cops too," Lucy whispered.

I smiled and rolled my eyes at her. "I was planning on it," I whispered back.

My eyes went back to Jason. "Maybe you can talk to my mom. She'll probably listen more to your opinions than she will mine."

Jason nodded. He knew that my mom trusted him, and had used that fact to talk me out of many sticky situations with her. That he was no longer my boyfriend would probably even add to his credibility, rather than detracting from it.

He looked from Chase to Lucy, then back to me. "Could I talk to you in private first?"

My mouth went a little dry at the suggestion. Most of the time, when people wanted to talk to you in private, it was nothing good.

"S-sure," I stammered.

Lucy's face held surprise as she looked at me, then stood. Without another word, she hustled over to take

Chase's arm, then dragged him out of the room with her.

I looked up at Jason warily, feeling strange that we were yet again alone together after so many weeks of near radio silence.

He approached the bed and took the seat my mom had formerly occupied, then scooted it a little closer so he could take my hand.

"It kills me that I wasn't there to protect you today," he admitted, not quite meeting my eyes.

I bit my lip, unsure of what to say. "It's not your job to protect me," I said softly.

He looked up from his lap. "I know, and according to you, it *never* was my job, but it doesn't stop me from wanting to do it."

My mouth opened in surprise. "I was never against you protecting me," I argued, "but you're right, it wasn't your *job*. I did my best to protect you as well, but it was because I wanted to, not because I was obligated."

Jason frowned. "That came out wrong. I guess I meant that it wasn't, *isn't*, my place."

I huffed in irritation. "It doesn't have to be your *place* to protect someone. You don't need to ask permission."

"Well if that's the case, then I should have been there today," he replied, catching me with my own logic.

I tried to think of something clever to say, but my brain felt numb and I was all out of wit. "I'm not your problem anymore," I mumbled, feeling like I might cry from frustration.

Jason's eyes widened. "You were never a problem, Xoe."

I smiled bitterly. "It seems to me I've caused you *plenty* of problems."

Jason looked down at my hand in his, then back up to my face. "Just tell me that it's okay for me to watch out for you until this is all over. I would never forgive myself if you died, and I could have stopped it. Once you're safe, we can figure out where my place is, if I even have one at all."

"I'm not going to die," I breathed, trying to lighten the mood, but Jason didn't take the bait.

He stared at me until I met his eyes. "We thought you were dead, Xoe. When we got here and they rushed you off on a gurney, it seemed like you'd stopped breathing. We had to sit in that little waiting room for thirty minutes before they came back out and told us you were okay."

I gulped. With my demon healing I was already feeling better, and death seemed a long way away. I tried to imagine how I would have felt if Chase, Jason, or Lucy were the ones being rushed away on a gurney. The thought made my heart hurt.

"I'm sorry," I whispered as a few retched tears leaked out of my eyes. "I didn't mean to put you all through that."

Jason squeezed my hand. "Just promise me you'll let me help. Just for now."

I nodded, not knowing what else to say. If Jason was in danger, I knew I would do anything I could to keep him safe, boyfriend or no. I couldn't really deny the same opportunity to him.

He nodded in return and stood. "I'll see what's taking your mom so long, not that I'm not grateful for the delay."

I nodded again. His hand slipped from mine, then I was alone in my little hospital bed, waiting for my mom to come back.

Quite some time passed before she walked back into the room, followed by two uniformed police officers, both women.

The younger of the two officers took a seat next to me and offered a warm smile. Her face was covered in dark freckles and she looked about sixteen, though I knew she had to be older. She had the perfect appearance for disarming a seventeen year-old who, for all they knew, had just suffered a traumatic attack. Unfortunately for them, I didn't feel traumatized. In my world, a few knife-wounds were child's play.

"My name is Molly," she began, still oozing warmth. "Do you mind if we ask you a few questions?"

"Go for it," I replied, trying to not sound as impatient as I felt.

The other officer, an older woman who stood off to

the side with my mom, gave a look of disapproval at my tone.

"What's the last thing you remember before you woke up here?" Molly asked, drawing my gaze back to her.

"I remember being in my friend's car," I replied evenly, feeling no need to go into detail since they likely already knew that I'd arrived in Jason's car.

"And where were you before that?" she asked just as sweetly.

My thoughts raced. We'd left from the alleyway, but my blood was probably still in the bathroom where Nix had cut me.

"I was in the bathroom of a restaurant," I stated, since the alleyway was a lot less likely to be discovered.

"Some pedestrians claimed they saw you being carried out of an alleyway," she said, as if surprised by my answer.

Crap. I hadn't thought to discuss things so thoroughly with my *accomplices*, and now I had no idea what stories they might have given the cops. Seeing no other way, I tried to stick as close to the truth as possible.

"I woke up in the bathroom with the knife-wounds," I said evenly, "then I went outside to find my friends. I was pretty delirious, so I must have wandered into the alleyway. I'm lucky they found me."

"Someone at the restaurant reported a large amount of blood," the older cop confirmed. "Yet it seems no one saw you leave the bathroom. I'm not even sure how you could have walked at all with your injuries."

I shrugged, feeling annoyed with my own foolishness. "I don't know what to tell you, officer. I didn't *teleport* to the alleyway, if that's what you're suggesting."

"And what do you remember about your attacker?" she asked, obviously dissatisfied with my answer.

I shrugged again. "I don't even remember being attacked. Maybe I hit my head."

The older cop raised an eyebrow at me. "Does the name Daniel Wilson ring a bell to you?"

"No . . . " I trailed off, having no idea why the cops would be asking me about someone named Daniel Wilson.

"He's presumed dead. According to several sources, you knew him," the officer went on. "Your name came up with a red flag."

Oh crap. They meant *Dan*, the crazy werewolf I had helped to kill . . . but there was no reason for my name to come up in the system. I had never even been questioned. The officer was lying, but why?

"What about Claire Nelson?" she asked when I didn't answer.

The gears in my brain clicked into place. We lived in a small town. Within a year someone had gone missing, someone had been murdered, and now someone had shown up with mysterious knife-wounds that probably looked similar to those found on Claire.

"I think I went to school with her," I said, playing dumb.

My mom glared at the cranky officer. "Is there a *reason* you're asking my daughter all of these questions? She's the victim of an attack."

The officer glared right back at my mom, not ruffled in the slightest. "Her wounds match up with those of three murder victims. I think your daughter was almost the fourth."

My eyes widened. So they knew about Ben and Sasha. Apparently witches weren't as good as werewolves about covering up murders. At least they suspected me as a victim and not as a suspect.

"My daughter needs to rest," my mom demanded.

The older officer puckered her lips in annoyance. Molly smiled and handed me a business card. "If you remember anything, please give us a call."

As soon as the door shut behind the two women, I turned worried eyes to my mom. *I need to get out of here*, I mouthed.

She approached my bed so she could lean close to my ear. "Xoe, *what* is going on?"

I took a deep breath. "Get me out of here and I'll tell you."

"Jason said the same thing, but you need to recover," she replied, her voice cracking with unshed tears.

"Mom," I said patiently. "I'm a demon. I'll be fine by tomorrow, and I don't need the doctors speculating on how I recovered so quickly."

My mom's eyes widened. "Oh *no.* I hadn't even thought about that."

Unwilling to leave me alone again, my mom pushed the little button to summon a nurse. The nurse was probably going to be pissed that she was getting called to my room when my mom should have gone to the front desk, but I didn't care. My mom was actually doing what I asked, and that was good enough for me.

Two hours and tons of paperwork later, I was being wheeled out into the well-lit parking lot of the hospital. I didn't feel like I needed the wheelchair, but I grudgingly decided to keep up appearances until we were out of the disdainful doctor's sight.

The doctor had argued that someone in my condition should not be going home, and that I needed to remain under *observation* for at least one more night. If only they knew what that observation might entail, they would have scooted me right out of bed, sans paperwork.

I didn't think Nix would come back to finish the job, but my grandmother sure would. Imagine the nurse's horror when she came back to find her patient drowned in a bowl of green jello. I'd take being filleted by Nix over getting knocked off by my grandmother any day of the week.

8

Everyone caravaned back to my mom's house, including Devin, who was still waiting for his turn to talk to me. Jason had called him, uneasy about leaving Emma unguarded to take me to the hospital. Abel was watching her now, and it was Devin's job to get the scoop.

We all gathered in the living room to discuss the event, when what I really wanted to do was sleep. Lucy and Allison had taken a post on either side of me when I'd first been allowed out of the hospital, and had stayed glued to me ever since. They rode with me in the back of my mom's jeep, and now they sat with me on the couch. If only their moral support could extend to handling the questioning that was about to begin, I'd be set.

Four dining room chairs had been moved to provide additional seating. Max had snagged the love seat, leaving Chase, Jason, Devin, and my mom to sit in the less-comfortable dining room chairs. Of course, my mom had almost instantly vacated her chair in favor of making coffee and snacks. I couldn't blame her for being uncomfortable in a room with several werewolves, a vampire, and two demons. Few humans would be. Allison was a *special* case.

"So tell me what happened with this demon girl," Devin began, pausing to take a sip of his coffee. He looked a little more ragged than usual, with wrinkles in his suit and slight bags under his eyes.

"Her name is Nix, and I just tried to talk to her," I explained, "and even offered to take her back underground, but she has a serious vendetta against the witches, and I think against me."

"Why you?" Allison asked. "You were both screwed over by the witches and your grandmother. You'd think you'd be on the same side."

I shrugged. "My grandmother had the witches torture her, then I show up, looking just like Alexandria, trying to stop Nix from killing any more of the witches. Draw your own conclusions."

"Looking just like your grandmother?" Max asked as he lounged comfortably on the love seat. He was wearing the pajamas he'd worn to visit me in the hospital, plaid pants with a baggy blue tee shirt. That he'd already been wearing them when I was attacked, around 6 pm, said a lot about how much he cared for appearances. He was the exact opposite of Allison.

I sighed, not really wanting to get into another explanation that had nothing to do with our current predicament. “Some of the more powerful demons don't age. My grandmother was centuries old, but only looked a few years older than me.”

“Geesh,” Max replied, “just when I thought demons couldn't get any creepier. Does this mean you won't age either?”

I rolled my eyes at him. “I'm tired so I'm going to overlook the creepy comment, but no, it doesn't mean I won't age. I'm half-human and will most likely live and die like the rest of you mortals.”

“Except for Jason,” Max countered, not letting the subject drop.

“Back to the matter at hand, *please*,” Devin interrupted in annoyance. “Do you think this girl will come after you?”

I turned my attention back to Devin, grateful for the interruption. “I'm not sure. I don't think she was trying to kill me, else she would have stayed to finish the job. My guess is she was just trying to get away from me at the time. Of course, now that she knows my grandmother is dead, she might change her focus.”

Devin answered with a curt nod. “Duly noted. Now I'll need the address of the witches who are tracking the demon girl.”

I looked at him suspiciously. “Why do I get the feeling that I shouldn't honor that request?”

Devin sighed just as my mom walked back into the room. "We're not going to *kill* them."

My mom let out a little *eep* of surprise. We all turned to look at her.

"I'm just . . . going to go upstairs," she said as she backed away. "Xoe can fill me in on everything later."

Everyone said goodnight and turned to get back to business, but I couldn't help watching her as she left. Things had finally gotten back to almost-normal between us, and now here we were discussing murder in her living room, right on the heels of putting her through a day at the hospital and police questioning. It didn't bode well for the future of our relationship.

"Way to freak out my mom, *Devin*," I chided as I turned back around.

He smirked. "I was asking for the address so we could take them into custody. You're the one that made implications."

I leaned back and sunk into the couch to pout. Chase and Jason eyed me, both abnormally quiet. I shook my head and turned my gaze back to Devin. I could only deal with so much at once.

"What do you mean, *custody*?"

It was Devin's turn to roll his eyes. "The demon girl wants the witches, and maybe she wants you. We already have you, so if we obtain the witches, the girl will have to come to *us*."

"Nix has been biding her time for over a month," I countered. "We might have to wait a while."

Devin cocked his head at me. "Okay, miss smarty-pants, what do you suggest?"

I sat up straight, not wanting to launch into my plan from my lower vantage point. "The witches are going to help us summon Chase's brother, Sam," I explained. "Sam can speak to the dead and has control over spirits, so he can help me with my little haunting problem."

"And what about the demon girl?" Devin pressed.

I crossed my arms and prepared to divulge a part of my plan I'd yet to share with anyone. "Sam's spirits can carry demons between realms," I explained, "and they can't get stabbed. Once the witches get a bead on her, we'll have Sam send his spirits to take her under. At that point, the demons can deal with her."

Devin crossed his arms, mirroring me. "And what makes you think that this Sam person will be so willing to help you?"

I smiled bitterly and moved my eyes to Chase. "Because he owes me, and helping me is a lot better than the alternatives." I didn't need to say out loud what those alternatives might be. The people in the room knew me well enough to catch on.

Chase met my gaze and nodded, affirming that my plan was relatively solid.

Devin clapped his hands together, suddenly pleased. "For once I don't have to do anything. I like it."

Jason cringed, which was the first sign that he was

actually paying attention to the conversation. He looked at Chase. Chase, looking back, nodded.

"Actually, I'm going to have to back out of the job with Emma," Jason announced. "I'd like to see this thing with the witches through."

I looked back and forth between Jason and Chase, wondering what the nod was about, but my attention was soon drawn back to Devin as he sighed dramatically.

He placed a hand over his eyes and shook his head. "My work is never done."

I snorted. "Sing it, soul sister."

He smiled at my joke and stood, then eyed everyone in the room in turn. "I'm going to head to my hotel for some rest. I imagine Xoe will be well taken care of in the interim?"

"Sir, yes sir," Allison and Max both said in unison. They turned and grinned at one another.

Jason smirked and looked at me. "And they said *we* were bad with the mushiness," he muttered.

I smiled in reply and looked back to Max and Allison, who didn't seem to notice the exchange.

Devin looked down at me. "A moment, if you would?"

I nodded and tried to stand, but Lucy had to give me a boost off the couch so I wouldn't strain my abdomen stitches. You never realize how much you use certain muscles until you can't.

I followed Devin outside onto the porch, then

waited while he shut the door behind us. I groaned as he walked past me toward the driveway, expecting me to follow. A closed door wasn't enough when you wanted privacy from vampires and werewolves.

The moon lit my way to Devin's car as he waited, holding the passenger side door open for me. Once I reached him, he had to hold onto my uninjured forearm as I tried to lower myself into the seat without bending my upper body. The movement still strained the stitches uncomfortably, but we managed. As soon as I was settled, he went around to the driver's side. The slamming of his door was startling, leaving us in the car alone, where my supernatural friends were less likely to hear our conversation.

"Why all the secrecy?" I huffed, annoyed to be in a freezing cold car instead of my warm, cozy home.

"I want to discuss this situation with the cops," he admitted as he gazed out into the darkness.

I sighed. "They lied when they questioned me. Said I was a person of interest."

He turned and raised an eyebrow at me. "How do you know they were lying?"

I snorted. "I'm not stupid. I've never even been questioned by the police. I wouldn't be a person of interest *just* for knowing Dan, and being in the same grade level as Claire."

Devin nodded. "They just see a girl with unusual wounds matching those found on multiple murder victims."

I frowned, not sure where our conversation was going. "So what's the problem then?"

Devin frowned too. "You're surrounded by a lot of violence, Xoe. The police may start investigating you, looking for something to link you to Claire and Sasha, and maybe even Dan."

"But I'm not doing anything illegal-" I began, but he cut me off with a raised hand.

"Not right now, but sometimes you do. If this demon girl attacks you again in public and you kill her, it will be hard to plead self-defense since her weapons are incorporeal. Harder still to explain how you lit her clothes on fire without a lighter or any form of accelerant."

I tried to shift into a more comfortable position, but ended up tugging on my stitches hard enough that it felt like they might tear. Perhaps the doctors were right about me staying in bed. Stitches were a real pain.

"So what do you want me to do?" I forced through gritted teeth, slowly shifting back to my original, hunched position.

Devin shook his head. "I don't know. This is why demons, even ones with a good portion of human blood, don't normally live in this world."

"So you're saying I shouldn't live here?" I asked, hating the shakiness of my voice.

Devin sighed and patted my shoulder. "No, in fact, you should spend as much time here as possible as long as the police are interested in you. Disappearing for long periods of time to the demon world will likely increase their curiosity."

Devin seemed deep in thought, thoughts he still wasn't telling me. There was more to his worry than the cops. I could sense it.

I waited for him to meet my eyes. "What is this about, really?"

He quirked the corner of his mouth. "Nothing gets by you," he replied tiredly.

I crossed my arms lightly so I wouldn't aggravate wounds. "I'm waiting."

He bit his lip, then turned to fully face me. "Abel would kill me for saying it, but I don't think you should remain in the position of pack leader. It's not good for you, or any of us."

My jaw dropped in surprise. "You guys have been pretty gung ho about me sticking with the job. Why the change of heart?"

Devin shook his head. "Things are not good for the wolves. The western packs are divided from the eastern, and beyond that, the East is divided between North and South. Conflicts between factions are increasing. The northeastern packs have taken to working with witches to give them an edge. They were the ones who inspired Abel to involve himself with demons. Demon trumps witch most every time."

I narrowed my eyes at him as the gears began to turn in my head. "I knew the reason Abel wanted me as a pack leader was to add the threat of demons. Why do

I get the feeling you're trying to tell me something *more*?"

Devin's face shut down. "I believe Abel intends to acquire more demons. His plan so far has worked. The other packs are afraid, but I don't think it will have the results he intends. When you back a wolf into a corner, it doesn't cower. It attacks."

"Like the pack that threatened the local witches," I observed.

Devin nodded. "They weren't rogues. They came here from Connecticut to knock Abel down a few pegs. No one wants to see more demons brought into the mix."

"Gee thanks," I muttered.

Devin shook his head at my dejected expression. "I'm not saying this to hurt you, Xoe, and I'm not lumping you in with the stigma surrounding demons. I'm saying that this is all making you a walking target. You need to stay here for now, but when things have settled down a bit, I think you should step down and move underground. *Permanently*."

I was too tired to be angry. Instead I gave him my best apathetic expression. "I'm a target down there too, don't you get it? I'm the only living demon who can make portals. Now that my dad is dead, there's nothing to keep other demons from trying to use me. The invading wolves were only a secondary danger in the plan that my grandmother, a *demon*, orchestrated."

Devin placed his hands on the steering wheel,

flexing his fingers in frustration. "So what will you do?" he asked finally.

I laughed bitterly. "I'll try to stay alive. Beyond that, I can't make any plans. My life is dictated by whatever the next emergency is. All I can tell you, is that I'm a lot more frightened of demons than I am of werewolves."

Devin stared through the windshield at the moon. "I suppose that's wise."

We sat in silence for several minutes.

Eventually I put my hand on the door handle to leave, but before I did, I turned back to Devin. "You know, you're a lot more serious when you're not around everyone else."

He smiled softly. "I've lived in a world where I've needed to hide my emotions for a very long time. Humor and sarcasm are great deflectors."

I smiled back. "Well, thanks for caring, at least."

He nodded. "You're a good person, in bad circumstances. You don't deserve to be forced into all of this."

I nodded, unsure of how to reply, then struggled out of the car and shut the door. I took a few steps back as Devin started the car, reversed it, then drove away.

You're a good person, he'd said. Sometimes, I begged to differ.

9

I walked back into the house to escape the cold. The painkillers they'd given me in the hospital were quickly wearing off, and my wounds, though partially healed, were beginning to ache even without movement.

Everyone was waiting for me, eating the snacks my mom had laid out. With Lucy's help, I returned to my place on the couch, feeling almost too exhausted to keep my eyes open. I glanced at the snacks, knowing I should eat, but not wanting to lean forward enough to fix myself a plate.

Sensing my discomfort, Lucy scooted to the edge of her seat and piled a paper plate with cheese, crackers, veggies, and ranch dip, then handed it to me. I took it gratefully and began munching away, waiting for someone to break the silence. Though I was exhausted, I would have really liked to get either Chase or Jason alone to ask about their seeming secret conspiracy regarding me. Maybe I was just being paranoid, but I sensed something amiss.

"I can't believe they tortured her," Lucy blurted out, breaking the morose silence. "What would they have had to gain?"

"Information," I answered, knowing she was referring to Nix.

I gave Chase a side-long glance. I hadn't discussed the folder of information that he'd found on my dad's doorstep with anyone else. My dad had been researching something long before he knew his life was in danger, and I had a feeling that Nix knew a little something about that.

Chase raised an eyebrow at me. "You have no intention of letting Nix go free in the underground, do you?"

Lucy looked back and forth between the two of us. "What information?"

I bit my lip, having an unexplainable instinct to conceal that news. "Nix knows something that my grandmother wanted to know, and my dad was looking for information before he died. That's reason enough for me to want to find out what's inside of Nix's head."

Allison raised an eyebrow and looked down at my bandaged arm. "Correct me if I'm wrong, but I'm guessing she isn't exactly the chatty type."

I put a piece of cheese on a cracker and bit down, deep in thought as I chewed. "She actually said quite a bit," I said finally, then frowned, "before she tried to slice me open. She might sing a different tune once we get her back underground."

"Are you sure this thing with Sam is going to work?" Lucy pressed. "It seems like you're putting an awful lot of faith in him."

"That's even if we can summon him to begin with," Chase added.

"I thought you were on my side," I pouted, turning my gaze back to him.

Chase sighed. "I am. I just don't like the idea of the witches drawing from you to do it. For all we know, Cynthia blames you for everything that happened and is plotting some horrible revenge."

"That wouldn't help her with Nix," I argued. "She needs me."

"That's not to say that the spell won't have some adverse effect later on. She only needs you until you get rid of her demon problem," he countered.

Jason's expression was pensive as he said, "There has to be another way. I don't think the witches should draw from you either."

I narrowed my eyes at him, then turned to Chase. "I'm guessing you filled him in on a few things?"

"Did you not want me to know?" Jason asked before Chase could answer.

"I think that's our cue to leave," Max announced as he stood.

Lucy and Allison stood as well. *Traitors*.

"Call and let us know what the plan is," Lucy

paused, then added, " . . . once you figure everything out."

I nodded, then turned back to Chase and Jason, ready to get to the bottom of their new-found alliance. They both stared back at me innocently.

As soon as I heard the door shut behind those who'd departed, I pursed my lips. "Care to tell me the plan you two have formulated?"

Chase cringed, but Jason remained straight-faced.

"We want the witches to draw from Chase," Jason explained. "They're afraid of you, so we need you at full power, should anything go awry."

My jaw dropped. "And what if they *are* just wanting to screw me over? They might hurt him instead."

"Better me than you," Chase stated.

I raised my eyebrows in surprise. "Says who?"

Jason raised his hand.

I snorted, not surprised that Jason would rather sacrifice Chase than me. "This is *my* deal," I stated, "so I decide who the witches draw from, and I choose *me*."

"We're summoning *my* brother," Chase argued.

"Then you should be the one at full-strength to deal with him," I argued right back.

Chase shook his head. "The whole point is to convince him to work with us on the grounds of making amends with you. He'll want a guarantee that you won't try to kill him. If the spell takes enough energy for you to lose consciousness, my promises won't be very convincing."

I opened my mouth to argue, but couldn't think of a way around the point he'd just made.

"You know he's right," Jason added, rubbing salt in the argument-losing wound.

I crossed my arms, then cringed at the pain of pressure on both my stomach and arm bandages. "I can't believe you both worked against me to sort this argument out beforehand."

Chase's expression softened. "I don't view it as working against you if we're trying to keep you from harm."

Jason rolled his eyes. "But Xoe does."

I opened my mouth to argue, then the power went out and everything went dark. I sat perfectly still, wondering what happened since there were no storms in the forecast.

I sensed movement, then a hand found mine, though I wasn't sure whose it was.

"Do you hear that?" Chase said from beside me, confirming whose hand I held.

"It's like a high-pitched whining," Jason answered from the general area he'd been when the lights went out.

I squeezed Chase's hand tightly in anticipation. I could feel an electric buzzing in the air that seemed to be mounting. Suddenly, I was deafened by the sound of shattering glass. I hunched over and covered my face reflexively. It sounded like every window and mirror in the house had exploded simultaneously. As the glass settled, I could hear my mom screaming. Something must have still been happening in her room.

"No," I whispered. I stood and pulled away from Chase to blindly stumble toward the stairs. Footsteps raced up the stairs ahead of me, letting me know that Jason had beat me to the punch. At least, I hoped it was him and not some unknown intruder.

My mom screamed again, propelling me forward. The stitches in my stomach strained as I threw myself up the stairs, but the tearing pain wasn't enough to stop me. I couldn't lose another parent. Not now.

I felt like I was moving in slow motion, even though I knew realistically I reached the top of the stairs in a matter of seconds. I ran down the hall, using my memory more than spacial awareness to keep from running into anything. As I neared my mom's room, a green glow became apparent. Jason stood in to doorway, silhouetted by green light.

Chase reached my side and we both stepped forward to peer around Jason in awe. The smaller pieces of furniture in the room floated on their own, occasionally popping and crackling with currents of static electricity. The green glow wasn't emanating from anywhere in particular, but was more intense around the floating objects.

I pushed past Jason and stepped into the room, too panicked to worry about the possible repercussions. My mom was nowhere to be seen.

I distantly felt tears dripping down my face, but I

couldn't seem to focus. Chase walked up behind me. I felt his hands land on my shoulders as Jason walked further into the room. He reached out to touch the floating lamp, then recoiled in surprise as it shocked him with a loud *zap*.

I pulled away from Chase, desperate for some clue to where my mom might be. My foot landed in something slippery and thick. I crouched down to look at the substance as my mom's cell phone floated by in front of my face. The stuff was dark and almost glittery, and somehow familiar.

I looked out across the carpet, illuminated by the green glow. There were more globs of the substance, some as large as my mom's slightly hovering bed. It also coated some of the furniture, seeming to radiate in intensity from a central point.

Suddenly it clicked. "The dream realm," I muttered, not fully understanding my own conclusion.

Neither Chase nor Jason seemed to hear me, too mesmerized by the odd scene.

I stood and cleared my throat, "A portal was made to the dream realm here. I've seen this slime before, the first time I went looking for my grandmother."

Chase's shocked expression looked strange illuminated by the green light. "How can that be possible? The only two demons that can make portals are you, and-"

"My grandmother," I finished.

"But she's dead," Jason argued.

I shook my head. "If she's the one haunting me . . . " I trailed off.

"You think she took your mom to the dream realm?" Chase asked, confused.

I shook my head, feeling numb. "I don't know what I think, but something either came from, or went to the dream realm from this room. There's no other way this goop could have gotten here."

Chase walked up to me and grabbed my hand. "Then let's go."

I looked around my mom's room. Everything was in disarray, but not the kind of disarray it would be in if I made my own portal in there. I couldn't use the same form of travel that I used between the underground and the human world. Traveling between realms required portals.

"Not here," I stated. "We need to go outside where I won't destroy anything more than trees."

Jason came to stand on my other side. "I'm coming too."

I looked up at him. I was nervous enough going back to that place myself, and actually didn't mind the extra company. "Are you sure?"

Jason nodded, though he really didn't look sure.

Not wanting to waste any more time, I took his answer at face value, and turned to leave the room. Jason and Chase followed me out into the hall and down the stairs, like tall, solemn shadows in the green light.

I didn't bother checking the electricity on my way down. The light bulbs were probably all toast anyhow. Instead, I felt my way blindly through the living room toward the front door.

We let ourselves outside. The night was peaceful and dark, with just the barest sliver of moon visible outside. The air was cold, but no colder than the icy pit of my stomach. As we walked across the yard, memories of my first dreamworld experience came flooding back. I shivered as I recalled the dark, ominous creatures, only visible in reflections, that preyed upon visitors.

Next my thoughts jumped to the demon I'd met who'd originally owned the ring that was stolen by my grandmother, passed on to my dad, then passed to me. The ring that still resided on my finger. The demon had tried to kill me, and Dorrie had come to the rescue, shoving her so hard that she went through a wall. Dorrie had done the same thing to my grandmother, only there was no wall to go through, and the fall had broken her neck.

Really, it would have been a good idea to bring Dorrie with us, but I couldn't risk anyone finding out that she'd left the dreamworld.

We left my yard and continued walking until we reached a more remote part of the woods. We stopped to look around, surrounded only by trees and the sound of chirping crickets. It was lucky that my mom's house was on the edge of the forest, so we didn't have to go far for such seclusion.

I took a deep breath, then lifted my hands away from my sides. Jason and Chase each took one, squeezing way too tight. I couldn't blame them for being nervous. We weren't just traveling to another place, we were traveling to an entirely different plane of existence.

"I'm going to aim for the correct plane," I explained, "but the dream realm is really confusing. We may end up somewhere else, in which case, we'll have to find a driver."

Not waiting for anyone to protest, I closed my eyes and thought of the eerie place in the dreamworld that looked like a scene out of *Dracula,* hoping that it was the only place that had the sparkly slime that was left in my mom's room.

I gritted my teeth as we were all flung upward. We popped out of existence, only to land in a jumbled heap on hard asphalt. I groaned and turned my head to see a lonely bench next to a flickering streetlight.

10

Chase crawled out of the dog pile we'd formed to sit a few feet away on the asphalt while he caught his breath. "You've gotten rusty at portal making," he observed.

I shrugged as I rubbed a sore shoulder. "It was never a very comfortable journey."

Jason, who'd moved to sit off to my other side, looked around warily. "Did we make it? This place doesn't look particularly *dreamlike*."

I looked over my shoulder at the empty bench, framed by the dark silhouette of the depot. The last time I'd seen the depot had been right after my dad died. I'd never figured out if it had been a dream, or if I had really been there, saying goodbye to my father.

"This is it," I replied, trying to keep my voice steady, "though we want a different realm."

Jason got to his feet and offered me a hand up. "I thought this was all one realm."

Feeling shaky enough to actually need the offered hand, I took it, then slowly rose to my feet. "It is, but there are realms within the realm, or I guess they're more like sections, divided by massive barriers. The sections aren't *actually* right next to each other, but the barriers make it seem like they are. Each time you go through a barrier, you end up in a place completely unlike the previous one."

Jason shook his head. "This is all beyond me. Just tell me how we find your mom."

I looked at the empty benches again and had a thought. "Normally, we'd need to wait for a cab, operated by a *driver* like Dorrie, but my grandmother could travel between sections of the dreamworld without portals, maybe I can too."

"How do you know that?" Chase asked, since he knew just about as much about my grandmother as I did.

"When I first met her, she found me in the section we're going to," I explained. "She poofed in, just like I can do between the demon underground and the human world."

"So you think you can poof us into the correct section?" Chase asked.

I nodded. "Maybe. I've been there before, so it's worth a shot."

Chase took my hand. "That's good, because I think something is creeping up on us."

I looked around quickly, then remembered the type of creatures that stalked the bus stop. Instead of looking at what might be right in front of us, I looked into the reflective glass of the depot. Sure enough, a huge shape loomed there, growing smaller in the reflection as it made its way toward us.

I held out a hand to Jason, shaking it in the air for him to take it quickly. Just as the shape closed in, I shut my eyes and thought of the place with the sparkly slime. We poofed out of existence, just as the creature lunged, narrowly missing us. Almost instantly we reappeared in the dark place I remembered from my adventure with Dorrie.

Chase released my hand and crouched to poke at a pile of goo on the ground. "You were right, Xoe. It looks the same as what was in your mom's room."

I nodded to myself as I dropped Jason's hand. We had ended up right in front of the house where I'd met the demon who'd tried to kill me. The mansion looked just as dilapidated as before, with its gate mostly overgrown with brambles and vines, barring the way inside.

"Where do we go from here?" Jason asked, looking around warily.

I shrugged, the slime was everywhere. There was no way to tell which part of the current realm the portal had come from.

"Mom!" I called out, cringing as my voice echoed throughout the barren canyons around us.

The mansion was the only house in sight, and I wasn't about to go inside to ask the crazy demon if she'd seen my mother. Instead, I walked away from the structure, calling out for my mom as I went.

Within a moment, Chase caught up to my side. "Are you sure yelling is such a good idea?"

I shrugged as I tried not to cry. "I don't know how else to find her."

I stopped and looked around the desolate landscape for some sign that my mom might have been there. If I ever got my hands on my grandmother for this, I'd kill her all over again. Hopefully then she'd stay dead.

I was just about to give up hope when I saw a green light in the distance, illuminating the inky black sky.

"Look!" I shouted in excitement, pointing in the direction of the light.

I began to jog toward it, though the terrain was uneven and often slippery with the shimmery slime. A moment later, Jason caught my arm, halting my momentum. I looked up at him with a mixture of shock and annoyance.

"It could be a trap," he warned, still gripping my arm.

I scoffed. "You know we have to go anyway."

He sighed, then in the blink of an eye was gone, running off ahead of me toward the light. I glared after him, then turned all of my focus to the light. A moment later, I was standing right beside it in a cloud of red smoke. The smoke looked ruddy and ugly against the green light, but did nothing to dampen my satisfaction in beating Jason to the finish line.

My satisfaction was short lived, however, as something shoved me to the ground, straight into a puddle of slime. I tried to get my arms underneath me, but the slime was incredibly slippery, and I only managed to lift myself up to my elbows so I could look over my shoulder. There was nothing in sight, except for a giant, slime-covered boulder hovering toward me, surrounded by the green light. The boulder's stony surface glistened, and would have almost been pretty if I couldn't guess at the boulder's intent. If it landed on me, I'd be crushed.

Seconds before the boulder finished its slow progress forward, Jason appeared. He grabbed my arm, tugging me to my feet and out of the way. The boulder lost its green glow and thunked to the ground. I had barely sighed with relief when a baseball sized rock lifted and sped toward us.

If it was just me, I would have been hit, but Jason's faster reflexes allowed us to dodge as a single unit. Several more speeding rocks came our way, and we dodged each in turn. Suddenly something hit us from behind, knocking us down, just as a volleyball sized rock whizzed by where our heads had been. Chase rolled off of us, then more rocks came speeding right for my head. Not even thinking, I held both of my hands out in front of me to ward off the blow.

Spurred on by my terror, energy gushed through my arms, erupting from my palms to form a solid dome of fire around our prostrate forms. I was so shocked that I almost let the fire go, but quickly refocused. The rocks bounced off the wall of flame like it was solid. It didn't stop whatever was controlling them, probably my grandmother, from trying, but we were temporarily safe.

Once it became clear that the rocks wouldn't work, the thing attacking us switched to launching bursts of pure, green energy at the fire. The bursts all came from a central point, and I somehow knew that was where my grandmother's incorporeal form was standing.

The green energy was repelled by the fire just like the rocks had been, yet each time another burst hit, I felt like it was scalding my skin. My arms began to waver as Chase and Jason huddled on either side of me, powerless to help.

I knew I'd have to let the barricade down soon, and our only hope was if I could somehow hit the incorporeal form before one of the rocks hit us. Even then, I might not be able to hit her at all. I was about to try anyhow, when a cloud of gray smoke appeared and barreled toward where the energy bursts were originating. As quickly as it appeared, the gray smoke was gone, as was the green light.

Not about to miss my chance, I let the wall of fire

down, grabbed Chase and Jason by their arms, then made a portal back to the woods behind my mom's house.

We landed in a heap again, and I had a few seconds to look up at the starry night sky before I lost consciousness.

I WOKE up in my bed to the sound of voices downstairs. I sat up slowly, hurting everywhere. My arms hurt especially. I turned on my bedside lamp to examine them. They were covered with long welts, some spanning several inches. The stitches were missing from my forearm, but the knife wounds were healed enough to stick together. The long cuts were no longer straight, deformed by the fresh burns. I lifted my shirt to examine my abdomen. It had healed as much as my arm, but the stitches were still present there, and the cuts were clean and straight.

I shivered as I remembered the bolts of green energy hitting my shield of fire. Even though the fire had protected us, a measure of the energy had broken through to scald me. It was unnerving, especially since normally I couldn't get burned at all.

I stumbled out of bed, hoping that it was still the night I had passed out on, and I hadn't slept through an entire day into the next night. I looked down to find that I was still covered in residue from the shimmery slime, then had to take a few steadying breaths to keep from losing control of my emotions. My mom was still lost in that place, and me breaking down would do her no good.

I rifled through my closet in the dark, delaying the sting my eyes would feel when I switched on the lights. Without much thought, I grabbed a clean, charcoal colored, short-sleeve blouse and black jeans. I'd be forgoing sleeves and sweaters that day, as the burns on my arms were too tender for coverage.

I went into the adjoining bathroom and washed the remaining traces of goop off my skin, using my night-light to see. I dressed, then took a deep breath, preparing myself to tell Jason and Chase that I was going back to the dreamworld for my mom, whether they liked it or not.

I left the bathroom, and was about to leave my bedroom as well, when I realized someone was sitting in a chair in the corner of my bedroom near the bath-room door. I about jumped out of my skin, until I looked a little closer in the dark. Max lounged in my desk chair, deep asleep in an uncomfortable looking position. Some watch-wolf he was.

I left Max to sleep and let myself out into the hall-way. I recognized Abel's voice and Jason's, and instead of going down the stairs to interrupt, I paused to listen. I didn't listen for long though as a woman interrupted what Abel was saying.

A rush of elation washed over me. "Mom?" I questioned loudly, not fully believing that she was only a room away.

"Xoe?" she questioned back. Her voice was a little closer, like she had moved toward the base of the stairs.

I rushed down the hallway and barreled down the stairs. Sure enough, my mom was standing there, completely unharmed.

I threw my arms around her as soon as I reached her. My burns screamed out in pain, but I didn't care. "How?" I asked weakly with my chin resting on her shoulder.

She pulled away from me. "All of my furniture started floating, so I ran and hid in my closet, only the stuff in the closet was moving too. I vaguely remember something hitting me in the head, then I woke up, left the closet, and saw my room covered in slime. When I searched the rest of the house, you were gone."

I gritted my teeth in frustration. My grandmother had tricked us. My mom was never in the dreamworld. I noticed blood in my mom's hair, and feared she might have a concussion. "You need to go to the hospital," I demanded.

My mom stepped back and nodded. "Abel was about to take me."

I sighed as I took in everyone else in the room. Abel was standing near the door, ready to leave for the hospital. Chase, Jason, and Lucy sat on the couch with Lucy in the middle, and Cynthia and Rose were smushed together on the love seat.

I looked at the witches in surprise. "What on earth are you two doing here?"

Cynthia wrung her hand in her lap nervously. "We came home from the grocery store to a trashed apartment. Someone had written *I'll find you* on the wall in ketchup. I tried to call you, but you didn't answer, so we came straight here."

I pinched my brow in annoyance. With all of the excitement, I had completely forgotten about Nix. I took a deep breath, preparing myself for the ordeal ahead.

First, I looked at Abel. "Take my mom to the hospital," I ordered. "After she gets checked out, bring her someplace safe. Have Devin corral my new pack members, and bring them here. It's time to pay pack dues."

Abel quirked an eyebrow, but didn't seem offended that I was ordering him around. "What are you planning?"

"This all ends now," I said with a cold smile. "I'm not going to be bullied by my grandmother's ghost, or by a demon girl with a chip on her shoulder. We're going to summon Sam *tonight*. First we'll take care of my grandmother, then we'll move on to Nix."

"And what do Emma and Siobhan have to do with any of this?" he pressed, still not moving to do as I'd bade him.

I glanced at Cynthia, who was quietly lecturing Rose for getting excited about summoning another demon. "Safety in numbers," I said, not wanting to say out loud that I wanted extra wolves there in case Cynthia tried anything after we took care of Nix.

Abel glanced at the backs of the witches in question, then gave me a slight nod before turning to my mother. "Shall we?"

My mom nodded and went to stand by the door with him. Before they left, she turned back to me. "This demon you're summoning is your friend, right?" she asked nervously. "He won't try to hurt you?"

"He's Chase's brother," I explained, avoiding the second question, since I really didn't know the answer.

Taking my reply at face value, my mom nodded and allowed Abel to escort her outside. A moment later I could hear a car start, followed by the crunch of tires on the gravel driveway. I breathed a sigh of relief. My mom was safer with Abel than with me. I was a living target.

How do you protect your loved ones when just being around you is a danger? Answer, you don't. You make someone else do it. I was hoping to do the same thing with Devin, Emma, and Siobhan. If I ended up incapacitated, I wanted my friends to stand a fighting chance.

If you want something done right, acquire worthwhile minions.

11

Devin had arrived with his two charges in record time. Siobhan was *not* happy about Emma being asked to come out in the wee hours of the morning when she had school to worry about. I had gently reminded her that if she had a problem with how I ran things, she could hoof it back to a larger pack where she'd have more responsibilities. She promptly shut up.

Emma, on the other hand, seemed elated by the whole situation, and was currently impersonating a cute, little jumping bean from her perch beside Lucy on the couch.

I was standing near Emma and Lucy, watching with my arms crossed as Rose and Cynthia poured salt all over my living room floor. At least they had the decency to remove the rug and coffee table, but the salt was still going to be a pain to clean up.

I turned my attention to Emma. "Why do I get the feeling that you have a million questions to ask right now?"

Her face cracked into a nervous grin as she touched her dark, curly hair self-consciously. "Is that a bad thing?"

I smiled in return, though on the inside I felt sick and nervous. "I was just going to say, if you have questions, feel free to ask them."

Emma's face lit up at that. "Why are they pouring salt on the ground?"

"The type of magic they're using might attract other spirits," I explained like I knew what I was talking about, even though it had just been explained to me moments before Emma arrived. "They need the circle to keep them from interfering."

Emma looked confused. "So it's not to keep the demon *in*."

I sighed, frustrated that everyone always assumed that all demons are evil. "That too," I answered grudgingly.

"Can *you* be summoned like that?" she asked innocently.

I ground my teeth, thinking back to the only time I'd ever been *summoned*, though in reality I was carried up from the demon underground by ghosts. "I could if I was in the demon world," I answered vaguely.

She looked behind her to verify that it was just us girls in the room. Jason, Devin, and Chase had gone to get supplies for the witches, and hadn't yet returned. "Is Chase's brother as cute as he is?" she asked in a hushed tone.

I was so stunned by her question that I laughed. She seemed so young, and I felt so old, making it hard to remember we were actually close in age.

Siobhan watched us like a hawk from the love-seat, curling her loose red hair behind her ear like a student in deep observation. It was a little unnerving, but good, I guess, that she paid attention when her ward started talking about boys.

"No," I answered, laughter still in my voice, despite the discomfort Siobhan was causing me, "but I'm biased because I hate him."

Lucy laughed too. "He *is* pretty cute," she commented, surprising me almost as much as Emma's question had.

Rose paused what she was doing and watched the exchange in awe, probably because we were talking about boys in front of her mom and another older woman. Though Cynthia seemed too distracted to pay attention like Siobhan was.

I would have pressed Lucy on the subject, making sure that she had no romantic designs on someone who'd set up my father to die, even if he'd done so unknowingly, but was interrupted as the boys finally returned from their mission.

Chase walked in ahead of the others. I moved out of the way so he could hand two plastic bags to

Cynthia. "It's not easy to find blue candles at 3 am on a weekday," he commented as Cynthia took the bags, then set them down so she could paw through their contents.

She seemed almost frantic as she pulled out five blue pillar candles and an enormous ball of twine, sweeping her unusually messy, chin-length hair off her face in irritation.

Jason approached and propped a large, simple-framed, wall-hanging mirror against the side of the couch, near where Cynthia crouched. I raised a questioning eyebrow at him in as Cynthia mumbled to herself, but he only shrugged.

Cynthia's nervousness made me feel jittery. I wasn't afraid of Sam, and she had no reason to be either, so why was she acting like we were embarking on a life-threatening journey?

Devin, who hadn't been carrying any loot himself, went into the kitchen and began grinding beans for coffee. It was a little rude of him to just presume he could use my kitchen, but it was also 3am, and I didn't think any of us were going to make it through the night without caffeine. We could have taken the time to rest, but I wasn't about to leave my grandmother another opening to attack.

I walked around the arm of the couch, side-stepping the mirror to take a seat beside Lucy. I nudged her over so Chase could sit on my other side.

Cynthia handed Jason the candles. "Place them

equidistantly around the salt circle," she instructed. She placed the mirror in the center, face up, handling it gently like it was a revered object. "The mirror serves as a doorway," she explained to the room in general. "It will allow him to come through without a full portal. The salt circle will keep him trapped."

I didn't feel the need to tell her that Sam could probably travel outside of the circle with the help of his ghosts, as I doubted he would. I didn't see him intentionally placing his physical form anywhere near me until he knew I wouldn't harm him. The circle would keep me out just as much as it would keep him in.

I clenched my jaw at the thought of being near him. It really rankled me that I'd have to work with a demon I really wanted to pummel, or worse. Sensing my tension, Chase put his hand on my knee and squeezed, hitting that uncomfortable ticklish spot with absolute precision.

I squirmed away from his hand, glaring at him.

"Snap out of it," he said with a wink. "We're one step closer to figuring everything out."

I took in a deep breath and let it out. "With the help of your brother . . . " I trailed off.

Chase looked at me apologetically. "I'm not terribly excited to see him either."

Lucy leaned forward on the other side of me so she could see both of us. "Do you really think he'll help us just to get Xoe off his back?"

Chase nodded. "He makes his living dealing information. He can't do that if he's in hiding and no one can find him to ask."

Lucy frowned. "So he'll help because it's cutting into his business, not because he feels bad or because he's your brother?"

Chase snorted. "Sam has never had much of a conscience. He only does something if it benefits him in some way."

Judging by Chase's bitter tone, I guessed that he'd learned that lesson with Sam long ago, and more recent events had only confirmed it.

"So why did he leave us that folder of information?" I asked. "I don't see what he would have gained from that."

Chase shrugged and frowned. "He's as unpredictable as he is self-absorbed."

I frowned too, glad for once that I was an only child.

Cynthia, who'd been lighting the candles Jason had placed, rose and cast me an impatient look, just as Devin came into the room with several mugs of coffee placed on a tray. He went around the room handing everyone a mug, then very deliberately handed one to me.

I looked down at the mug, then laughed, seeing it was the one with a picture of a raven on it. The scrawled words beneath it read, "raven lunatic".

He shrugged with a smile. "Seemed fitting."

I smirked, not offended by his little jest since it lightened the mood of the situation.

Cynthia sipped her coffee, then sat cross-legged next to the mirror. "Xoe will need to be part of the circle," she explained to everyone, as if to avoid eye contact with me. Curiouser and curiouser.

"We were actually going to have you draw from me," Chase cut in.

Jason eyed me steadily from where he stood near Cynthia, daring me to argue.

"But you're not as powerful as her," Cynthia argued for me. "It might not work. Alexandria was stronger than either of you, and it fatigued even her."

I had an idea, one that Chase and Jason hopefully wouldn't be able to argue with. "What if you draw from both of us? Would that prevent me from becoming incapacitated?"

Cynthia's face scrunched in thought, emphasizing the heavy bags under her eyes. "It might work. You'd likely at least remain conscious."

Rose, who had gone to sit by Siobhan, either not realizing that she was a werewolf, or not afraid of her regardless, cleared her throat. "I can help too, then no one will pass out."

"Absolutely not," Cynthia snapped instantly.

Rose crossed her arms, not noticing that doing so invaded the bubble of personal space between her and Siobhan even further. "*Mom,* there's a circle. I'm not going to be in any danger."

Cynthia shook her head, looking almost panicked again. "That's what we thought with the other demon."

"Yeah," Rose argued, "but Xoe's grandmother let that one out, and she's not here."

Cynthia glanced at me, and I suddenly understood what she was worried about. She thought I'd pull the same thing as my grandmother, and free the summoned demon.

"You *wanted* me to be unconscious for this," I accused.

Cynthia cringed, then finally met my eyes. "Can you blame me?"

I really couldn't. She'd lost her daughter and husband because of my grandmother, and here I was, looking just like Alexandria, with the same sort of powers, making Cynthia summon another demon.

I slumped back against the couch cushions, feeling defeated. "What would make you feel better about this?"

Cynthia's eyes widened in surprise. "The fact that you asked that is a good start."

I mentally slapped myself. I could be such a bulldozer sometimes, oblivious to how it might affect people. She didn't trust me because I did more ordering than asking.

"You can draw all of the energy from me," I said finally. "I'll go to sleep and you'll have nothing to worry about."

"*No*," Chase and Jason said in unison.

Cynthia shook her head and held up her hand to silence them. "No, it's okay, I'll draw from both of you. Rose can help."

I was momentarily stunned by her sudden change of heart. Who knew being nice to people could be so beneficial? I'd have to try it more often.

I gave her a genuine smile. "Thank you."

She nodded, seemingly unsure of her offer, but she didn't rescind it.

Chase and I both stood. "So what do we do?" I asked.

Max chose that moment to come stumbling down the stairway, still looking half asleep with his sandy hair sticking out in all different directions around his freckled face. He went to stand next to Jason. "What did I miss?" he asked groggily.

"A lot," several of us said in unison.

He shrank back at our tone. "Geez, I see all of you woke up on the wrong side of the bed."

Lucy smiled sweetly at him. "Most of us haven't even been to bed yet, you slacker."

Max shrugged. "I take my naps where I can find them."

Cynthia cleared her throat and stood, drawing our attention back to her. "We'll need to sit around the circle," she explained. "Xoe," she said, finally looking at me, "you'll be to my right since you'll provide more energy than Chase, and my right hand is dominant. Chase will be to my left, and Rose will sit across from me. We'll tie the twine around our wrists and use it to link our hands since we won't be able to reach each other with how large the circle is."

"Why can't we just hold the twine?" I asked, not liking the idea of being tied together.

"If one of you still ends up losing consciousness, you might let go," she explained, sounding far less nervous than before. "We need to keep the circle solid."

"Okay," I conceded, placing my mug on the end table next to Emma. I took Chase's and did the same. "What will everyone else do?"

Cynthia shrugged. "They just wait and jump in if things get out of hand."

Devin, who'd been listening from the sidelines, grabbed a pair of scissors from the little table where my mom and I usually left our daily belongings, then rejoined us to retrieve the ball of twine. "How long?" he asked, referring to the twine.

"Two feet each should be good," Cynthia replied. "We'll need four strands."

"I *can* count," Devin mumbled under his breath, but Cynthia either didn't hear him, or chose to ignore him.

She took a seat outside the salt circle, facing inward. Chase, Rose, and I joined her. I watched Chase from across the circle, reminding myself that this was all just as hard on him. It was easy to forget since he didn't show it.

Devin handed us each a piece of twine, then he and

Lucy set to helping everyone tie one end of each piece around our wrists.

Devin leaned close to me as he tied mine loosely, so as not to agitate my burns. "Are you sure about this?" he whispered.

I nodded, though really I wasn't. Not because I was afraid of Sam, but because if he wasn't willing to help, I wouldn't know what to do next. This *had* to work.

"What is the demon's full name?" Cynthia asked once we were all secured and Devin and Lucy had stepped away.

"Samuel Agne," Chase replied.

Cynthia nodded in acceptance. "Rose and I will both envision the name. It's better to envision the demon's appearance, but as we've never seen him, the name will have to do."

"So should Chase and I visualize his appearance?" I asked.

Cynthia shrugged and closed her eyes. "It can't hurt."

I was about to question whether or not she knew what she was doing, then I felt a strange tugging sensation. Kind of like being in a wind tunnel, except the sensation moved in two directions at once, and there wasn't actually any wind. My natural instinct was to fight against the tugging feeling.

Cynthia opened one eye to look at me. "You have to let us draw your energy or it isn't going to work."

I gulped, then nodded hesitantly. I hadn't thought

about what it might feel like to give my energy to someone, and I was pretty sure I didn't like it.

I closed my eyes in an attempt to calm my racing heart, and this time when the tugging came, I pushed energy back at it. The energy flowed outward invisibly, and I was pleased to find that I could control how much I gave, at least for the time being.

Cynthia and Rose gasped as the energy hit them. There was a little bit of spillover from the other side, letting me know that Chase was contributing as well. His energy felt different than mine, cool and reserved where mine was fiery and unpredictable.

I pictured Sam in my mind's eye. First I saw his dark hair, similar to Chase's, but surrounding a slightly more rugged, wide face, then I moved down to his eerie whitish eyes. He was shorter than Chase, but most people were. I started to feel groggy, but not exhausted enough to pass out.

The energy built until there was a loud *pop*. I opened my eyes in surprise to see Sam standing within the circle next to the mirror. What I could see of the mirror's surface swirled with gray mist that emanated slightly above the glass, like the mirror was casting its own reflection.

Sam whipped around, looking confused. His eyes found me before they found his brother. He cringed. "You really went to the extent of hiring witches to kill me?"

I sighed tiredly, because it hurt to have to say what I

was going to say next. "I'm not going to kill you," I grumbled.

He looked around the room at those who now occupied the couch and love seat. "Then why did you bring so many werewolves? Nice to see you again, by the way," he added. Since he was looking over my head I knew he was looking at Lucy, and she was probably blushing right back at him.

I lifted my hand as far as the twine would allow and snapped my fingers to regain his attention. His gaze turned back to me as he waited for me to speak.

"Don't you want to know *why* I'm not going to kill you?" I asked.

He took a seat beside the mirror, lounging casually as much as the salt circle would allow. "Yes, do tell."

"I want you to help me get rid of my grandmother's ghost, and I want you to help me drag the demon she loosed back to the underground."

Sam's eyes widened in either fear or surprise, maybe both. "I am not going anywhere near your grandmother's ghost. Ghosts that can make portals are not good. She's been terrorizing the dreams of everyone who ever wronged her."

My arms erupted in goosebumps. Though I had been pretty sure all along that it was my grandmother's ghost messing with me, having a solid confirmation gave me the heebie jeebies.

"We have a way of locating you now," Chase said from behind Sam. "Being terrorized by a living demon who can make portals might be worse than being terrorized by a dead one."

Sam smiled bitterly. "Why brother, you're here. I thought I smelled a *snake*."

I snorted. "We all know who the metaphorical snake is in this situation."

Sam grinned. "Yes, but I don't have fangs."

"Bully for you," I replied sarcastically. "Now back to my grandmother."

"The other demon is a more simple matter," Sam replied. "I can send some of my spirits to snatch her up right now. Where do you want her?"

I raised an eyebrow, surprised at how easy he made it sound. "Somewhere she can't escape?"

Sam nodded, seemingly deep in thought, then his face split into a grin as he started laughing. "I really had you going there. I can't just snatch demons out of the human world. They have to go willingly."

My jaw dropped in surprise, then I glared at him. "Maybe I *will* just kill you."

He tsked at me, the laughter melting from his face as if it had never existed. "Now, now. Though I don't want to go up against even a dead Alexandria, if it will allow me to return to business as usual, then I believe we can work something out."

I really, *really* wanted to pummel him, and judging by Chase's expression, he wanted to pummel him even more, but we both resisted.

"*How?*" I demanded.

"I want your promise to leave me alone first," he demanded right back.

"*Fine*," I replied, feeling like the answer betrayed something inside me.

He grinned. "Shake on it?"

"You can't," Rose interrupted, "not with the circle intact."

Sam looked over his shoulder at Rose. "Why hello there," he said, doing his best to be charming.

Rose blushed and tried to reach up to push her red hair out of her face, but the forgotten twine stopped her

"Don't look at her," Cynthia snapped, drawing Sam's attention to her instead.

"You could have chosen a nicer witch to work with," Sam commented.

I gritted my teeth, annoyed with the entire conversation. "You know if we let you out, and you have your ghosts carry you away, we'll just have to summon you again."

He smiled, looking harmless. *Yeah right.* "This deal is mutually beneficial, and if I have your word that you won't try to harm me, I have no reason to run."

"Xoe," Cynthia cut in. "You promised we wouldn't let him out."

I gave Cynthia what I hoped was a reassuring smile. "He won't hurt anyone, and I can't take care of your demon problem until I take care of mine."

Cynthia glanced at Sam, then looked back to me,

still worried. "You'll still get rid of her, even though your original plan won't work?"

"If you can locate her, I'll take care of it," I promised, though I didn't enjoy the thought of seeing Nix again while I still had stitches from our previous encounter.

"And you'll keep your werewolf friends from harming Rose?" she added.

I raised my eyebrows in surprise. "Why would they hurt Rose?"

Cynthia glanced up at Devin, the only one of the wolves who'd stayed standing. "There have been threats."

I looked at Devin too. He shrugged, which meant yes, he had threatened her, and no, he wasn't sorry.

I turned back to Cynthia. "I wouldn't have let them hurt you regardless."

She let out a sigh of relief, then reached her hand toward the salt circle. "We have to break the circle before we cut the twine, else he'll just get sent back."

Not waiting for a reply, she swiped her hand across the salt. I felt no magical shift, but Sam was able to step out of the salt circle and over the twine that bound mine and Cynthia's wrists. He casually went to sit on the couch, forcing his way between Lucy and Emma.

While I glared at Sam, Devin approached with the scissors to cut us free. I held out my arm for him, but my attention was drawn back to the mirror still on the floor before he could make the first snip.

It began to shake all on its own, like something out of a horror movie, rattling its frame against the wood floor. We watched in awe as it began to emanate a green light.

"Cut the twine!" I shouted, able to take a guess at what would come next.

Devin rushed toward us and cut the twine between Rose and Chase, but the mirror continued to shake.

"That should have ended it," Cynthia gasped.

Devin freed both my hands. I stood and walked toward the mirror. "Everyone get out of here," I demanded.

Chase approached the mirror from the other side. The light was growing, and started to ooze out of the mirror like smoke.

"Break it!" Cynthia shouted.

Chase lifted his foot, ready to stomp his shoe down on the surface, but I stopped him with a raised hand. "Look," I instructed.

As we watched, the green was slowly shoved aside by gray, like a weak storm converging with a stronger one. The gray gave one final shove, then was gone, leaving the mirror's surface clear and still.

I looked over my shoulder at Sam, who still lounged on the couch. "Any idea what just happened?"

"Why Xoe," he began like I was being silly, "you didn't really think your father's death would stop him from watching over you, did you?"

The news hit me like a ton of bricks. I wavered

slightly on my feet. Chase moved to steady me as everything clicked in to place. The sink incident, with me suddenly being let free, then all of the light bulbs exploding, the gray smoke pushing aside my grandmother's incorporeal form in the dreamworld, and now with the mirror. It had been my dad, saving me every time.

I looked up into Chase's dark gray eyes as he came to all of the same realizations. "He saved us," he whispered.

I nodded with tears in my eyes. "I know."

12

While half the people in the room didn't know what was going on, the other half remained in sympathetic silence. Eventually I took a shaky breath and pulled away from Chase.

"I'm not going to let my dad spend his whole afterlife chasing my grandmother," I announced. "We are taking that witch out *today*." Realizing there were two actual witches in the room, I added, "No offense meant on the witch comment."

"Your grandmother is the reason Rose and I are in this mess to begin with," Cynthia stated, though she seemed hesitant. "If there's any way I can help you get rid of her, I will."

"Well then I hope you're okay with visiting the dreamworld," Sam interrupted as he tried to put an arm around Lucy.

She growled at him. The arm, knowing what was good for it, retreated.

I leaned near Emma to retrieve my now cold cup of coffee while keeping my eyes on Sam. "What do you mean?"

"Ghosts can only exist in this world partially," he explained. "More powerful ghosts can pull little tricks here or in the underground, but that's about it. When someone like me comes along to control a group of them, more meaningful tasks can be accomplished. Yet, the ghosts still aren't fully here, because pieces of them are in the dream realm. It's why people most often see strange things when they're near sleep or upon waking. They're closer to the dreamworld where those things reside."

"So if we chased my grandmother away from here," I began, putting together what he was saying, "she wouldn't be harmed and could just come back, if only in part. If we hurt her in the dreamworld, she will actually be hurt."

"Bingo," Sam answered with a crooked smile. "Fortunately, we have someone who can make us a portal there. I've always wanted to see what the dreamworld was like."

I raised an eyebrow. "You mean your ghosts can't take you?"

Sam shook his head. "Not to an entirely different world, and I have no talent for *dreaming*."

I actually had a talent for *dreaming* in addition to

my ability to make portals, though I saw no reason to give Sam any more information on me than he needed. It usually happened without my control regardless, and came in the form of sudden premonitions. It was my dad who'd explained to me that my premonitions were linked to the dream realm.

"It's not really a fun place to be," Chase added coolly. He was acting a lot more hostile toward his brother than I was, but I couldn't really blame him for not wanting to play nice.

Sam sighed dramatically. "Not only do you get to hang out with scary fire demons, they take you to other realms. No fair."

Instead of replying, Chase just glared at his brother. I couldn't help smiling a bit at the *scary fire demon* comment. It was a lot better than some of the other things I'd been called.

I was beginning to feel *really* tired, both from the small amount of sleep I'd had and from the energy it took to summon Sam, so I sat down near the salt circle. "I've only managed to take two people through a portal at once. I'm not sure if I can take more than that."

"So take two, come back, and grab two more," Sam suggested.

"That would be fine, except-" I paused, not knowing how to put into words that if we needed to leave suddenly, I'd only be able to save two people.

"We had to leave in a hurry last time," Jason explained for me. "If there had been more than two of us, someone would have ended up crushed by a boulder or annihilated by a ball of pure energy."

Sam wrinkled his nose. "That sounds . . . unpleasant, but I don't think we need to worry too much. Though my ghosts can't transport people between realms, they could help us escape to another area of the dreamworld."

I almost laughed as I realized my near fatal mistake. *I* could have popped us to a different area of the dreamworld too, instead of avoiding boulders and making a wall of fire that completely drained me of energy. I was still used to not having a quick, easy way out of situations. Old habits die hard.

Chase smiled wryly at me, obviously coming to the same conclusion. I held up my finger in a shushing gesture as I fought the blush growing on my face.

Sam shook his head. "I'm not even going to ask what *that's* about. When shall we leave?"

"Now," I said, at the same time Chase said, "Tonight."

I gave him a look of betrayal.

"We all need to rest, Xoe," he argued with the look.

I crossed my arms. "So my grandmother can attack again while we're unconscious?"

He mirrored my movements. "So we can face her while we're weakened with slower reflexes because we didn't get any sleep?"

I rolled my eyes at him.

"Don't the rest of us get an opinion on this?" Lucy interrupted.

I gave her an angry look, though my anger wasn't directed at her. "Only those of us going to the dream realm get an opinion, and the one making the portal retains veto power."

Lucy's eyes widened. "Who says I'm not coming!"

Before I could answer, Chase looked down at Lucy. "You can't come. If something happens to Xoe, you'll end up trapped in the dreamworld forever."

I gasped and turned my attention back to Chase. I hadn't considered that extremely important detail. "Well then you can't come either!"

"You can't go alone," Jason interrupted, drawing my attention over to him.

"Maybe not," I replied, "but I'm not risking you, Lucy, or *Chase*." I glared at each person as I said their names, emphasizing my point. "Can you imagine being stuck in that world?" I turned back to Jason, "especially as an immortal?"

"I don't see anyone worrying about *my* safety," Sam mumbled to himself.

I snorted at his sarcasm. "You said you *wanted* to go."

"I also *want* a back up plan," he replied, mimicking my tone.

I lost a little bit of my steam at that. "And do you have one you'd like to share with us, perhaps?"

Sam leaned back and put his arm around Lucy

again, looking smug. Lucy glared at him and scooted forward so his arm would fall back to the couch cushion.

Unfazed, Sam looked up to me. “Your pet witches pulled me out of the underground. Maybe they could pull us out of the dreamworld. If only demons go, we can all be rescued. Have your werewolf friends keep an eye on them to make sure they follow through.”

He was talking about Rose and Cynthia like they weren't there, which was unfortunately very *demon* of him. Most demons spent the majority, if not all of their time in the underground, and they could be fairly elitist, viewing races with relatively short lifespans as beneath them. Yet, it was funny that Sam would act that way. He and his brother's bloodline was so muddled that they might only live a human lifespan themselves.

“We barely managed to pull him from the underground,” Cynthia said, looking at me and ignoring Sam. “Without you and Chase to draw from, there's no way we could pull you from what you claim is an entirely different plane of existence.”

“Humans are more connected to the dreamworld than they are to the underground,” Sam explained, finally acknowledging Cynthia. “Even with the added barriers, the actual task should require about the same amount of energy.”

I shook my head. “She already told you she needed extra demon energy to make the summoning work. Who is she supposed to draw on if we're not here?"

"Werewolves have innate magic," Sam replied casually. "Have them draw from half of the wolves, while the other half . . . guard them."

"I'm not sure our type of magic is what Cynthia and Rose will need," Devin chimed in, finally joining the conversation.

Sam scoffed at him. "You have enough magic to provide supernatural strength, speed, and hearing, *and* you shapeshift. Do you have any idea how magically taxing shapeshifting can be for demons or witches? When it comes right down to it, you have far more energy than the rest of us. It's just more innately part of you, as opposed to something you willingly wield."

I looked to Cynthia for confirmation and she shrugged. "It's plausible."

Before I could say anything else, Sam cleared his throat to regain my attention. Once I met his eerily pale eyes, he began anew, "I'll stay here while the wolves and witches play nice to figure out what they can and cannot do, and you and my brother can go snuggle up somewhere to get some shuteye."

I'm pretty sure I had never blushed more than I blushed in that moment. "What makes you think that we'd go snuggle up?" I asked hotly.

Sam rolled his eyes. "Please, I know my brother. He wants to snuggle up with you. I'm just trying to help him out."

I could feel everyone's eyes on me, including Jason's.

"This is why I never want to ask for your help," Chase sighed.

Sam turned his attention to Chase. "You're asking for it now, little brother. You don't get to pick and choose what form it comes in."

I really didn't want to take the time to rest, but I wanted even less to remain in my living room with all of the tension now in the air. "I'm going to bed, *alone*," I announced. I turned to Cynthia. "Figure out if what Sam suggested will actually work, then get some sleep yourself?"

Cynthia nodded. I looked at Devin, who nodded without me having to say anything. He would hold down the fort. Abel would keep my mom safe. Everything would be fine. Now all that was left was for me to ride my unicorn up to my magical cloud bed, in a world where things actually worked out how they were supposed to.

I left everyone to plan, and went up to my room, cursing Sam under my breath. The situation was awkward enough without his comments, and I just knew now that he was aware he'd struck a nerve, he'd continue doing it.

I shut and locked the door behind me, then thought better of locking it. If my grandmother attacked me again, a locked door wouldn't keep her out, and would only serve to delay anyone who came to the rescue. *If* anyone came. It really was stupid of me to go to sleep by myself.

I unlocked the door and cracked it a bit, then flopped down on my bed. Hopefully someone would at least hear me scream. It would have to do.

I had only been lying on my bed for a few minutes when someone knocked on the door frame. Not waiting for a reply, Chase stepped into view as he pushed the door the rest of the way open.

I groaned. "Now they're all going to think we really are snuggling."

"Is that so bad?" he asked with a small smile as he came to stand at the foot of my bed.

I cringed. "It just seems . . . insensitive."

Chase crossed his arms. "Jason and I already discussed it."

I shot up in bed so fast it made me dizzy. "You *what?*"

Chase shrugged, then sat on the foot of the bed. He looked just as tired as I felt, and had dark circles under his gray eyes. "He doesn't want to date you right now, and I do."

My eyebrows shot up. "Well that was blunt."

"Do you want to date me?" he asked calmly.

I opened my mouth to answer, then closed it. "I, um-"

Chase looked at me steadily, waiting for an actual reply. When I didn't answer, he looked slightly hurt. "Well then . . . " he trailed off.

I sighed, feeling silly. “Of course I do. You just caught me off guard.”

He smiled. “So then, what's the problem?”

I cringed, “I just feel like it's insensitive.”

“It's been nearly two months since you guys broke up, and the breakup was mutual.”

“It's still weird,” I sighed. “We're trying to figure out this whole friendship thing, and I'm not even sure we can be friends.”

“Is that the whole reason?” Chase asked. “If it is, then that's fine, take all of the time you need, but I get the feeling that there's something else.”

He waited for me to answer, but I wasn't sure how to put what I felt into words. “I'm scared,” I said finally.

His expression softened. He looked almost hurt again. “Of what?”

I shrugged and looked down at my lap, feeling embarrassed.

I felt the bed shift, then suddenly Chase was sitting right beside me. He put his hand over mine. “Please tell me.”

I let out a shaky breath. “I'm afraid of everything changing,” I said, my voice barely above a whisper. “I'm afraid of you moving out of my dad's house, and things getting weird. I'm afraid of going to the only place I really feel at home and finding it empty. I'm afraid that if I screw things up between us, I won't belong anywhere at all.”

"You don't feel like you belong here, with your friends?" he asked softly.

I looked up at him as I fought against my tears. "How can I belong here? I'm part of a werewolf pack, but I'm not actually a werewolf. It's a danger for humans or witches to even be around me. My very existence seems to be driving my mom insane. When I'm in the underground, I don't have to worry about anything else. I know other demons can hold their own. If someone attacks me down there, I don't have to worry as much about collateral damage."

Chase began gently rubbing my shoulder with his free hand. "Your friends and your mom want you here," he assured. "You're an important part of their lives."

"Am I?" I asked, feeling almost hysterical. "Because it seems like they've all been living their lives while I've been too busy just trying to *stay* alive. They're finishing high school, making plans for the future. Allison and Max started dating and I didn't even know it. I have no future. When I'm here, I feel like I'm just going through the motions until everyone moves on without me."

Chase put his hand on my chin so I would meet his eyes. "*No one* wants to move on without you, Xoe."

I shook my head and looked down again. "No one has to *want* to. That's just life. It happens. They're going to go to college, get careers, get married and have babies."

"You can do all of those things," Chase said, sounding somewhat perplexed.

I looked up and raised an eyebrow at him, though the effect was probably dampened by my tears. "Trust me, marriage and babies are not my immediate concern."

"But college?" he suggested. "You can do that."

I shrugged. "That's just the thing. I really can't see myself doing that. I can't see myself trying to live a normal life."

Chase watched my expression carefully before saying, "You can live in the underground just as easily."

"And if you're not there, what would I do?"

He scrunched his eyebrows, once again thrown off by my line of thinking. "Why wouldn't I be there?"

I sighed. "Because if you date me, I'll drive you away. I'll be stubborn, and I'll argue. I'll recklessly endanger myself without ever asking your permission. I'll continue to run a werewolf pack, even though it puts me in more danger than I'm already in. You'll end up hating me, then I'll just be living in the underground alone, without any connection to the life I had there with you and my dad."

"Xoe," Chase began patiently. "You already do all of those things, and I'm still here."

I met his eyes. I tried to let what he'd said make me feel better, but it didn't. Tears began to stream down my face more steadily. "I can't lose anyone else, and I can't lose the last connection to my dad I have left."

Chase smiled sadly. “I take it I'm that connection.”

I rolled my eyes at him. “You're much more than that, you idiot, and you know it.”

He laughed and hugged me. “That's the sweetest thing you've ever said to me.”

I pulled away and smiled at him, feeling better even though nothing had been fixed. “Haven't you heard? I'm quite the romantic.”

He kissed me, and all of my worries about things changing came rushing up in an attempt to ruin it. I shoved them back down, because there was no stopping change. Sometimes change came at you with a bouquet of roses, and sometimes it came with a baseball bat. It was good either way, because if change never comes for you at all, you're probably dead.

13

I woke up with a start. Chase was sleeping right beside me. I guess Sam had been right after all. I rubbed at my eyes, trying to recall the dream I'd had. A dream that I wasn't sure was actually a *dream,* yet it wasn't like my other premonitions.

Everything had been foggy and hard to see, but I could tell I was lying on my back in the dirt. Someone was shaking me and screaming my name, but I couldn't answer them, because I was somewhere else. Somewhere dark and cold. Then I woke up.

I looked at the clock on my bed. It was already noon. We'd slept a good portion of the day away. I poked Chase in the arm. He swatted at me, but didn't fully wake up, so I poked him again. Finally he opened his eye a sliver and looked at me with the other half of his face still mushed into the pillow.

"Time to leave the dreamworld," I said with a smile, "to go back to the dreamworld."

He sat up and rubbed his eyes, spilling the blankets around his lap. "Speaking of dreams, I just had a strange one."

That caught my interest. "Go on."

He gazed off, as if trying to remember. "Everything was really foggy, and the fog intermingled with Sam's ghosts, who were flocking around us. You were on the ground, and you wouldn't wake up. I kept screaming your name, but you wouldn't move." He visibly shivered at the memory.

My jaw dropped, leaving me without words.

He looked at me, confused. "What is it, Xoe?"

I cringed. "What does it mean when two people have the same premonition?"

He drew back in surprise. "I don't get premonitions, Xoe. That's your forte."

I shook my head with worry. "If you don't get premonitions, then why did you have the exact same dream as me?"

His eyes widened. "The *exact* same?"

I wrapped my arms tightly around myself, feeling suddenly cold. "Everything except the ghosts. I didn't see the ghosts, but I was lying on the ground in the fog. I could feel someone shaking me, and hear them calling my name, but I couldn't wake up."

Worry saturated his dark gray eyes. "Maybe it's a sign that going into the dreamworld is a bad plan."

I shook my head, making my messy hair fall forward into my face. "There's no way to know the circumstances that lead to something happening. It might happen if we *don't* go."

He just stared at me, frowning.

"What?" I prompted.

"Xoe," he began hesitantly, "you wouldn't wake up. I can't go through that in real life. We have to figure out what the premonition means, and why we both had it."

I drew my eyebrows together in consternation. "Any suggestions on how we might do that?"

He sighed in frustration. "No, but-"

I held up a hand to cut him off, already knowing that he was once again going to argue our trip to the dreamworld. "Premonitions usually aren't literal, so I don't think we should worry too much yet. Right before my powers first manifested, I dreamed of fire, but in reality the first thing I did was burn Brian. Around that same time Lucy got scratched by a werewolf, but I didn't dream of her becoming a werewolf, there were just wolves howling in my dreams."

Chase looked at me like he didn't quite believe me. "And what could you lying in the dirt, completely unresponsive and perhaps dead or dying symbolize?"

"That I need to get more sleep?"

He didn't smile. "Don't joke, Xoe."

I sighed and dropped my head forward to rest against my palm. "I don't know what to tell you," I groaned. “We just have to do what we must, and hope for the best.”

“How are we going to eliminate your grandmother?” he asked abruptly. “We made plans to get there, but nothing after that.”

I shrugged. “I'm hoping Sam can help us find her, and maybe use his ghosts to help us get rid of her. My fire was able to stop her attacks, so maybe it can hurt her.”

“About that wall of fire,” he began, “I take it you've never done that before?”

I smirked. “You know for a fact that I haven't.”

“Just checking,” he confirmed. “I think it means that your abilities are progressing.”

“Come again?” I asked, not liking where his train of thought was going.

“Demons progress over time,” he explained. “It's why older demons are much more frightening than younger ones. They've had time to acquire their full range of powers. You've progressed a little more quickly than the norm.”

I narrowed my eyes, confused. “I really can't do that much.”

He looked at me like I was being silly. “First, you acquired the ability to *dream,* as you stated with your premonitions. Then you burned someone on contact, and soon enough you could create and control your own fire. You can touch hot objects without getting burned yourself, you can create portals, and you can *travel* like your father did. Now you create entire walls of fire, something I never saw your dad do. I'd say that's a lot."

"And what about your progression?" I asked, feeling embarrassed and wanting to take the subject off me.

He shrugged. "I've had a poisonous bite since birth, and when I was sixteen, I discovered I could breathe under water."

I held up my hand. "Hold the phone. You can breathe under water? How did I not know this?"

He had the grace to look abashed. "You didn't ask. I found out in a situation where I would have otherwise drowned. The story that goes along with it doesn't paint a very pretty picture of me."

"Oh?" I prompted, knowing that he probably wouldn't tell me. Chase was never forthcoming about his past.

"It doesn't matter," he replied quickly. "You've gotten us completely off topic."

"What else can you do?" I prodded playfully, not wanting to go back to discussing our shared dream.

He crossed his arms and gave me one of those patient, but really not so patient looks. "Nothing. It seems I'm all tapped out."

"Well maybe more will still come," I suggested. "In Hinduism, Nagas were said to have carried the elixir of life and immortality, and in Buddhism they could shift between human and serpent form. In most traditions, they're also viewed as protectors."

Chase raised his eyebrows in surprise. "How on earth do you know all of that?"

Realizing I had given myself away, I blushed. "I did some research when you first told me your mother was a Naga."

"*A lot* of research," he corrected.

There was a knock on the door, which at some point had gotten closed. "Are you guys just going to hang out in there all day!" Max called out.

I gave Chase a conspiratorial smile, then climbed out of bed. "Yes!" I lied, as I started searching my closet for fresh clothes. A shower would have been nice, but we'd already tarried long enough.

"Well then you're not getting any pizza!" Max called back. The sound of his retreat down the stairs followed.

I looked at Chase, who still sat on the bed. He shrugged. "He's got us there."

"That he does," I said playfully as I grabbed a dark green sweater and faded charcoal jeans from my closet. Without another word, I headed into the bathroom to get changed. Once I was alone, I let out a shaky breath. I would never admit it to Chase, but our shared premonition had me worried too.

I hadn't lied when I said that my premonitions usually weren't literal, but I normally only had them when something bad was coming. They were a warning. It did not bode well.

I brushed my teeth and washed my face quickly, trying to ignore my thoughts, then pulled my hair back into a ponytail. I'd been spending enough time in the underground the past few months that the lack of sun had made my hair slightly less white, and more of a honey blonde. It had also grown well past my shoulders, and could now be pulled into a ponytail without any strands coming loose.

I got dressed, then hiked the sleeves of the sweater up to the elbows, revealing my rapidly healing burns.

With a huff and a final look in the mirror, I left the bathroom so Chase could take his turn. His spare toothbrush was in my little toothbrush holder where he'd left it.

Chase was still sitting on my bed, waiting patiently. He caught my hand as I tried to walk past him to go downstairs.

I looked down at him in question, but he was looking at the burns on my arms. "They seem to be healing like a normal injury," he observed distantly.

His words didn't explain the worry on his face, but I knew what it was about. I felt almost guilty not outwardly sharing in his concerns, but it wouldn't help things if I did. I lived most days with death being a real possibility, so it wasn't like anything had changed.

I forced a smile. "They should be gone all together

in a few days." The unsaid thought hung heavy in the air, *if we even survived a few days.*

I pulled my hand away from him and patted his shoulder in reassurance. "I'll see you downstairs."

He nodded but made no move to stand. I left him that way, sitting on my bed like a forlorn puppy, as I let myself out into the hall.

The smell of pizza and sounds of conversation filtered up the stairs as I prepared to descend. I went down as quietly as possible, in hopes of sneaking by and heading straight to the coffee pot.

My hopes were soon dashed. Max spotted me from where he sat on the couch. "*Finally,*" he said, mouth half full of pizza.

I glared at him, then hurried toward the kitchen. Everyone was present and accounted for, including Jason and Sam, who sat in the dining room away from the others, discussing something in hushed tones. I was surprised to even see Allison and Lela, though I supposed it made sense at least for Lela to be there. Allison had probably weaseled information out of Max so that she could include herself in the action. I still wanted to inquire about Lela and Siobhan's past, but they seemed to be playing nice, so it could wait until things had settled down.

I made my way into the kitchen without further interruptions, only to find a completely empty coffee pot. I sighed, then grabbed the carafe to fill in the sink. At some point I had lost my fear of going near water, probably somewhere between getting slashed open by Nix, and almost getting crushed by a boulder in the dreamworld. Having someone try to drown me seemed almost pleasant in comparison.

Lucy and Allison met me in the kitchen as I poured fresh beans into the grinder. They both waited to speak until the grinder was finished and I had the coffee brewing.

Lucy, as usual, got right down to business. "We tried a small spell while you slept," she explained, "and it worked. Cynthia can draw from any of us just like she did with you and Chase."

I raised an eyebrow at her. "I really hope you slept at some point as well."

She nodded. "Most of us went and stayed at Allison's, while Sam, Devin, and Jason stayed here. We got back an hour or two ago to test things out."

I turned a tolerating smile to Allison. Her shoulder-length, honey blonde hair was held back from her face by a sparkly silver headband. The headband matched the clear crystal jewelry she wore, standing out in stark contrast against the magenta top that hugged her curves.

"And what are *you* doing here?" I asked, suddenly feeling like a fashionless bumpkin next to her.

She smiled right back. "The witches are going to need to draw from Siobhan, Max, and Devin. Devin wanted an extra person to keep watch with Lucy and Emma."

I tried to be mad, but the smell of coffee was wafting up my nostrils, easing the tension in my shoulders, and making me feel more at home. I realized at some point that I'd given up on keeping Alison safe from paranormal politics. She was intent on being a part of things, and really, who was I to stop her?

"So we're all set then?" I asked.

Lucy nodded. "We figure we'll give you a set amount of time, and if you don't return, we'll start pulling you out one by one."

I nodded in reply as I opened the fridge to grab the creamer. "Make sure you pull me out last. I don't want anyone getting stuck when I can travel on my own."

Lucy sighed. I looked at her in question. "Even Sam? I think we should pull you out before him."

"I thought you said he was cute," I teased as I poured my coffee. I gestured toward her and Allison with the coffee pot. They both nodded, so I put it down and grabbed two more mugs out of the cabinet.

"He *is* cute," Lucy defended. "He's also insufferable."

I smiled. "I'm glad to hear we share that opinion, at least."

Allison gave me a mischievous grin. "I seem to recall Xoe, that you initially found Chase insufferable as well."

I glared at her as I handed her a mug of coffee. "Don't go giving her any ideas. I'd hate to have to kill her boyfriend."

"I thought you said you weren't going to kill him," Lucy cut in, surprise clear in her voice.

I sighed and took up my cup of coffee to keep my emotions from boiling over. "I'm not going to," I admitted. "I wouldn't kill Chase's brother, but it doesn't change the fact that I really, really want to . . . *hurt* him."

"I can hear you, you know!" Sam called from the dining room.

Lucy's face erupted in a blush. Oops. I had completely forgotten that he and Jason were sitting so close by.

"And I think Lucy is cute too!" he added, not commenting on the *insufferable* part, while at the same time proving himself to be just that.

I rolled my eyes while I waited for Lucy and Allison to fix their coffees, then led the way into the living room. Chase had joined us. He was sitting on the couch next to Max. Siobhan and Emma were in the love seat, while Cynthia and Rose sat cross-legged on the floor. Devin paced in the corner, talking on his cell phone, most likely to Abel, who was hopefully somewhere safe with my mom.

I took a seat next to Chase, then scooted him over so Lucy could sit beside me. Allison sat on the arm of the couch next to her.

I handed Chase my coffee. He took a sip, as I leaned forward to grab a piece of pizza from the box on the floor in front of me. Next to the box, a new salt circle had been poured, and fresh candles had been set.

I took a bite of my pizza and looked to Cynthia. She looked slightly more clean and well-rested than the last time I saw her. “So remember,” I began, pausing to take another bite of pizza, “you're just the plan b. It might take us some time to do what we need to do. Don't jump the gun and pull us out early.”

Cynthia frowned. “I'm not sure this will even work.”

“That's why you're the plan b,” Chase commented as he stood. I looked up at him with a questioning eye. “Your coffee needs more cream,” he explained. He walked around the couch and disappeared into the kitchen.

Cynthia shook her head and met my eyes. “If something happens to you. The others could be stuck there forever.”

I could hear footsteps approaching the back of the couch, then Sam said from right behind me, “Worried about the welfare of demons? How sweet.”

Cynthia frowned again and looked past me to Sam. “I've seen what one demon's *vengeance* can do. I don't want any of your relatives coming after me if things don't go as planned.”

“Chase is my only relative,” Sam assured, “and little Xoe is the last of her line. Wipe us all out and there will be no relatives left. Of course, you might have to deal with our ghosts.”

I looked over my shoulder and glared at Sam. "You're not helping."

He raised an eyebrow at me. "And you're all delaying our journey. Let's get a move on."

I turned in my seat to face him more directly. "Why are you so anxious to go?" I asked suspiciously.

He rolled his eyes. "Believe it or not, I've got other things to do besides dealing with your big bad grandmother. I'm a very busy man."

Chase walked up beside his brother and held my coffee cup out to me over the back of the couch.

I tossed my half-eaten piece of pizza back into the mostly empty box, then took my coffee back from Chase. The coffee didn't seem to have any more cream in it, but I didn't question it. I took a deep swill, thinking that the coffee tasted a little odd, then stood. "Let's get this over with."

Sam thrust his fist into the air. "That's the spirit!"

Chase took a step away from his brother, looking a little green. "Are you sure we have to bring him?"

I sighed. "We don't want a replay of what happened last time. We need his ghosts to trap her."

Chase nodded and clasped his hands behind his back. He started humming softly to himself, letting me know that he was nervous.

Devin stopped talking on his phone just as Jason came into the living room to join the group. Everyone stared at me, waiting.

"Let's go?" I suggested weakly.

Sam nodded excitedly.

Devin came to stand by my side. "I'll walk you out."

Jason stepped forward. "As will I."

Lucy and Allison both looked unsure.

"I'll be fine," I assured them.

They turned toward each other with worried expressions. The room filled with tension. Finally, Lucy looked back to me. "If you don't come back, we'll find a way to get to you. No matter what."

I didn't have the heart to point out that if I couldn't make it back on my own, I was probably dead. Instead I smiled down at her. "I know."

Sam led the way to the door, followed closely by those of us going outside. We would return to the secluded area in the woods for lift off. I might not be able to protect myself or my friends, but I could at least make sure that no innocent passersby got caught in the destruction my portal would cause.

We all went outside, Sam practically skipping ahead of us.

Devin walked on my left as Chase and Jason fell behind. "Don't take your eyes off him," Devin whispered, nodding in Sam's direction.

I stared at Sam's back. "I don't plan on it."

"When this is all over," he began, his hesitant tone drawing my attention to his face, "I'd like to ask you a few questions about ghosts."

My eyebrows lifted in surprise. "I'm not exactly an expert."

We had walked across my back yard and entered the woods. Devin offered me a hand over a large, fallen tree. His blond hair whipped about in the cool breeze, partially obscuring his abnormally pale face. He looked even more tired than the rest of us.

"But you can communicate with them, at least in some way," he continued. "Especially in this dream-world I've heard so much about.

I inhaled slowly as realization dawned on me. "You want to contact your mom," I said softly.

"It's as good a way as any to find out if she's still alive."

I let out a deep, shaky breath as we ventured on. "Does Abel know you want to do this?"

Devin shook his head. "When we were unable to locate her initially, the subject was dropped. I dropped it along with everyone else, at least outwardly. That was, until you encouraged me to keep looking."

"Did I?" I asked distantly, recalling our conversation.

Devin had come to speak to me not long after my dad died. He'd shared the horrible story of his childhood, which ended with his dad being killed by a rogue wolf, and his mom disappearing. I had told him not to give up.

"I'll talk to Sam about it, once this is all over," I offered. "If anyone can find a specific ghost, it's him. You know it wouldn't be her entirely though, right? Just a piece of her residual energy. What my grandmother is doing is kind of immortal demon specific."

We had almost reached the clearing. I wanted to somehow comfort Devin, but we really didn't have the time.

He looked over at me sadly. "A piece of energy is all I need to know whether she's alive or not. If she's dead, I'll be able to let her go."

I nodded. He was being much more adult about the situation than I was. If I could find a way to hold onto my dad, even in ghost form, I was going to take it.

Sam came to a standstill ahead of us, directly where I had made the portal that brought Chase, Jason, and I to the dreamworld the previous evening.

He spun in a slow circle, marveling at the felled trees and soil looking like it had been scoured by one hundred mile per hour winds. He looked over at where I stood with Devin. "Your portal must really pack a punch."

Devin chuckled. "So does the girl herself."

I snorted and stepped forward to where Sam stood, then looked over my shoulder for Chase. He walked forward, leaving a sullen looking Jason to stand on the sidelines.

I looked over at Sam, not wanting to touch him, let alone hold his hand. He made the move for me, reaching over and gripping my right hand tightly in his own while Chase intertwined his fingers with my left.

I turned my attention to Devin, who had been

joined by Jason. "How long do we have before Cynthia starts pulling people out?"

"Three hours," he replied.

Three hours. It wasn't a lot of time. Hopefully Sam's ghosts would be able to find my grandmother quickly. If we got pulled out too soon, we'd just have to travel right back.

I cast one final glance at Devin and Jason. "You should probably step back a little further," I instructed.

They silently did as I bade, but still remained to see us off.

I closed my eyes and thought of the spot in the dreamworld where my grandmother had ambushed us. I felt the portal forming, but seconds before we were thrust upward, I heard a yell from Jason as someone jumped on my back. I would have fallen face first into the dirt if the portal hadn't already started tugging us upward.

I was overcome by the sickening feeling of rushing skyward, but at the same time felt weighed down with Chase, Sam, and some unknown person clinging to my back. I had never traveled with three people, and was overcome by the sudden fear that we might not make it all the way. We might get stuck in between planes, and I didn't know what we might find, let alone if we would survive it. I opened my mouth to scream, but my breath was stolen as we rushed out of existence.

14

We hit the ground with a thud, forcing up a cloud of stale dirt to surround our prostrate forms. Sam and Chase had landed on either side of me, but I had somehow flipped to land on top of our mysterious piggy backer.

I looked around as I struggled in vain to sit up, wanting to get away from the still body beneath me. The shiny slime and withered trees surrounding us confirmed we had hit our mark instead of ending up at the bus depot, but I had a feeling we'd just barely made it there.

A feminine groan at my back spurred me into action. I rolled to my side, then allowed Chase to help me to my feet. I looked down to see Nix, semi-conscious. Her shoulder-length, dark hair was a mess, and the back of her black, holey jeans and ratty white tee shirt were caked in dust from our impact.

Sam moved to my other side, looking down at Nix. “Who on earth is that?”

I sighed. “We're not on *earth* anymore, and that is Nix.”

Upon hearing her name, Chase put his arm in front of me and pushed me backward. I gave him an affronted look, but he didn't apologize.

“You said she cut you open with a flick of her hand,” he explained. “We probably shouldn't stand close to her.”

Fully coming to, Nix sat up. She turned her head and saw us. She almost fell back to the ground when her surroundings became clear. Once she regained her balance, she stood abruptly to face us, though she still seemed unsteady. “Where am I?” she asked sharply. “What did you do?”

I snorted. “*You're* the one that jumped on me, remember?”

She shook her head rapidly. “I thought you were going after your grandmother. I heard you talking about her. You lied about her being dead.”

I crossed my arms. “You were spying on us?”

She looked momentarily worried, then a tough expression overtook her face. “So what if I was? You still lied about her being dead.”

I rolled my eyes. “You're not a very good spy.”

She wrinkled her nose like she smelled something bad. “What is that supposed to mean?”

I glanced around, just to make sure we weren't

being crept up on, then turned back to Nix. "I'm being haunted by her ghost. I'd explain more, but one, we're on a bit of a time crunch, and two, you tried to kill me, so I really don't feel like explaining *anything* to you."

I turned to walk away, dismissing her. Chase and Sam complemented the gesture perfectly as they turned to walk on either side of me.

"Wait!" Nix shouted, jogging to catch up to us. "You can't just leave me here."

"Sure I can," I replied, keeping my eyes forward. I wanted to ask Sam to summon his ghosts, but I was afraid Nix would somehow interfere.

"If you want to get rid of your grandma's ghost, I can help," she said hurriedly. "I owe that old lady some of the hell she put me through."

I stopped and looked at her. Knowing I would somehow end up regretting it, I asked, "How can you help?"

She narrowed her eyes at me. "I'll tear her to pieces."

I laughed, though it sounded forced. "She's a *ghost*, she has no body to tear."

Nix's expression fell at that, and she went silent.

Not wanting to waste any more time, I sighed. "Just stay out of the way, and I'll take you back when we're done."

Her dark eyebrows raised in surprise. "R-really?"

I nodded. "Sure."

I would take her back all right. All the way to the

underground, but there was no reason to specify that out loud.

I looked to Sam. "Can you find her?"

He didn't reply, and instead closed his eyes. The energy he began to channel made my arms erupt in goosebumps. Nix gave him a worried look and took a step back, hugging her arms tightly around herself.

His ghosts weren't as apparent as they were in the demon world. In fact, when I looked directly at him, I couldn't see anything at all. The only way I could tell they were there was by looking out the corner of my eye. When I did that, I'd catch little glimpses of foggy figures swirling around Sam. He extended his arms and they all shot outward, searching.

I stepped closer to Chase, feeling shaky and sick with anticipation. My grandmother had nearly wiped us out during our last encounter. The only difference now was Sam's ghosts. If they weren't strong enough to hold her . . .

A sound like a thunderclap in the distance drew my attention just as Sam collapsed. I turned to watch him as he fell to his knees, clutching at his midsection. I looked back in the direction of the noise to see an eerie green glow lighting up an impossibly large expanse.

"Not good," Sam spat through gritted teeth.

Nix stepped away from us like she might run, but stopped herself. There was nowhere to run to.

I gazed at the green glow, then quickly turned back

down to Sam. "What's happening?" I asked breathlessly.

"She's fighting them," he groaned. "We underestimated her."

"We should go," Chase said quickly, looking off in the direction of the glow. It seemed to be growing nearer.

I shook my head, not wanting to give up, but knowing I probably should. The decision was made for us as the green glow suddenly leapt across the barren countryside, then closed in. With the glow came a dusty mist that abruptly obscured my vision and made it hard to breathe. I grabbed Chase's hand, then lifted the collar of my shirt to cover my mouth and nose as the dust grew thicker. It didn't leave me a free hand to summon a flame as we were suddenly enveloped in near darkness.

I maneuvered Chase's hand in mine to hold onto the belt loop of my jeans, still holding my shirt over my face with my other hand. Once he had a firm grip on me, I lifted my now free palm and summoned a flame. It was small, and didn't offer much light, but at least I could see Sam and Nix, who'd both stepped close to us.

What I could see of Sam's face looked white as a sheet. "She killed my ghosts," he panted, holding up his sleeve over his nose and mouth to filter out the dust.

"How can she kill ghosts?" I shouted through my shirt, catching his meaning.

He shook his head a little too quickly, his pale eyes wide with fear. "I don't know what she did, but they no longer exist. At least not on this plane."

"This isn't good," I whispered back harshly. There went our entire plan.

I extended my neck forward so my shirt would stay in place, let my flame go out, then held out my hands to Sam and Chase. "We should go. Nix, you'll have to piggyback again."

Nix nodded, then moved to stand behind me. She wrapped her arms tightly around my shoulders. Her closeness made me feel uneasy, but I doubted she'd stab me when I was her only hope of leaving the dreamworld.

I closed my eyes and imagined the edge of the demon city, somewhere where my portal wouldn't cause too much destruction. I couldn't go back to the woods if I wanted to trap Nix. I waited for that familiar rushing feeling, but nothing happened. Starting to panic, I threw caution to the wind and thought of the woods. Still, nothing happened.

I opened my eyes, then immediately had to squint against the dust. "Crap."

"Why are we still here?" Sam asked, sounding almost angry as he pulled his hand away from me.

Nix stepped away from my back. "She's neutralizing your magic, Alexondra."

I turned to face her, and wanting to stay close, Sam

and Chase turned with me. I reformed the fire in my hand, then looked at Nix expectantly.

Instead of looking at the fire, she looked down at my hand that still held Chase's. "Your ring is glowing," she commented.

I lifted our joined hands so I could look at my ring. The red stone was swirling with colorful lights, and the vines that composed the band looked almost like they were moving.

"I think you're somehow drawing power from the ring," Nix explained. "Maybe a portal takes more power than the ring can conduct."

Before I could reply, the dust began to thicken around us. We were either going to have to move, or be suffocated. Wordlessly we all agreed to join hands, and Chase led the way forward. I felt uneasy holding Nix's hand, knowing what she could do with it, but I didn't have the heart to leave her behind. I could only hope that Sam was trailing behind her, since I could no longer see more than a few inches in front of my face, and that was only when I dared to squint my eyes against the abrasive air.

We continued forward blindly. I felt Nix stumble behind me, then suddenly her hand was gone. I tugged on Chase to stop, but when I crouched down to find her, there was only emptiness.

"Nix?" I called out through my shirt. The muffled word was unintelligible, but maybe the sound would be enough.

There was no reply.

"Sam, are you there?"

Still no reply.

Chase tugged on my hand until I stood, then started walking forward again. He was right. There was no use standing around in hopes that we'd find Nix and Sam. They were probably already headed in another direction, searching for a way out of the dusty fog.

We walked on for what seemed like hours, but was actually no more than twenty minutes. I felt like I wasn't getting enough air in my lungs, yet there was little I could do about it.

Chase suddenly jerked on my hand *hard*, nearly pulling my shoulder out of its socket. At first I thought he was trying to hurry me forward, but then he jerked again so violently that I lost my hold on him. I stumbled forward, reaching out with both hands to find him, but there was nothing there. I was alone in the near darkness, barely able to breath.

Something shoved me in the chest so hard I fell onto my back. I couldn't hear anyone approach, but someone grabbed my feet and started dragging me. Realizing that the person wasn't there to help me, I began to struggle, but it's hard to free yourself with your feet lifted off the ground, and rough soil skinning your hands and elbows.

I tried in vain to brace my hands against the ground, but whoever had my feet kept tugging and my hands fell out from underneath me. The back of my head landed on a rock, causing stars to explode behind my raw, itchy eyelids. I felt warm blood seeping into my hair. I tried to look at whoever had my feet, but my eyes were closing against my will. In a last ditch effort, I used all of my strength to summon a ball of fire, then threw it in the direction of my feet. The lower half of my body dropped to the ground, but I couldn't seem to move. As I laid prone in the dirt, my eyelids finished their slow journey downward. Once they were shut, they refused to open again.

I WOKE to the sound of someone calling my name, but it was distant, like someone was calling from a far away cliff. I took a shaky breath, realizing that the dust was gone. In fact, my lungs felt fine. I sat up and looked at my surroundings. I was no longer in the slimy, dark area of the dreamworld. Instead, I was enveloped in a thick mist, but it was a pleasant mist, like being in a sauna, only it wasn't hot. It wasn't cold either. In fact, I couldn't feel the temperature at all.

I held up my hand in front of my face, flexing my fingers hesitantly, wondering if I was dreaming. I raised the back of my head from the soft soil, then moved my hand to touch the base of my skull. No blood.

I sat up with a start. The scrapes that I'd just incurred on my hands and elbows were gone, as were all of my previous injuries. I *had* to be dreaming.

I sensed movement behind me and jumped to my feet. I felt like I should have been dizzy, but I felt fine. A dalmatian sat a few feet in front of me, panting happily. The white parts of his fur were squeaky clean, making his black spots stand out in contrast. He looked up at me, and if I didn't know any better, I'd say he was smiling. Since I was apparently in a dream, I really didn't know any better.

He barked once and I jumped as the sound echoed around us. It sounded like we were in some sort of cave, though the mist was too thick to see any walls.

Once I slowed the racing of my heart, I glared at him, at least I thought it was a *him.* "I really hope this isn't some sort of premonition," I said to the dog, "because I have no idea how to interpret being in a misty cave with a dalmatian."

He wagged his tail and barked again, then stood and trotted off.

"Wait!" I called as I began to jog after him.

Though the mist obscured anything in the distance, I could see enough to tell I wasn't going to run into any walls or trip on anything. The dog was a foggy shape running ahead of me.

I felt oddly light as I ran, and my lungs didn't burn with exertion. There was what seemed like daylight ahead of us, probably the cave opening. The dog barked again, but kept running.

I was almost to the exit when something grabbed the back of my shirt. I had so much momentum going that my feet and arms continued forward as my upper body was held in place. Whatever held my shirt released its grasp, and I fell to the ground, landing solidly on my back, knocking the breath out of me.

I felt the first real sensation I'd felt since waking up in the cave. I stayed on the ground motionless, slowly relearning to breathe, as I listened to the sound of the dog's toenails clicking on the stone floor, returning him to my side.

I glared up at him as he panted above me. "You better not have had anything to do with that," I rasped.

He barked again.

"Get out of here, you mongrel," a voice said from my other side.

I recognized the voice that I hoped was speaking to the dog and not me. This strange dream suddenly had me experiencing a whole new range of emotions.

"Dad?" I questioned weakly.

He came to stand over me, looking just like he had when he was alive with his blond hair pushed back, and his bright green eyes staring at me intently.

I would have previously thought that it was impossible to pass out when you were already dreaming, but that's exactly what I did.

15

Something warm was on top of my lap. I reached a hand out blindly to find soft fur and little, floppy ears. I was leaning against something hard, and I felt cold. Extremely cold. I forced my eyes open to find I was still in the cave, with the dalmatian resting his head in my lap. The mist seemed to have subsided somewhat, but I still couldn't see the other end of the cavern.

I looked to my left at the presence I felt there. My dad looked back at me sadly, sitting with his back against the wall next to me.

"Are you real?" I asked. "I had a dream about you before, and I still wonder whether or not I really spoke to you."

"Both were real," he replied as he let out a shaky breath, "but only one was a dream."

I scrunched my eyebrows at him in confusion. "I don't understand."

He put his hand on top of mine, yet resting on the dog's head. "You're dead, Xoe."

I looked around the cavern in confusion, then back to his worried face. "No, that doesn't make sense."

"You were killed in the dreamworld," he explained. "That demon girl shoved you, and you hit your head on a rock. The blow cracked your skull."

"Nix?" I questioned, still not fully grasping the situation. "Why would she shove me?"

My dad scowled. "She's been working for your grandmother, terrorizing those witches to make them leave town. I don't think the girl intended to kill you though."

I wasn't so sure about that. "This wasn't the first time she attacked me," I explained, "and Alexandria has tried to kill me a few times as well. That was obviously her goal."

My dad shook his head. "I don't think the girl knew that. She's a particularly viscous specimen, and I've no doubt she would have killed you right away if she thought that's what she was supposed to do. My guess is your grandmother hasn't been able to communicate with her, so she assumed you were to remain alive until your grandmother could enact whatever she had in store for you."

"So Alexandria had some sort of plan in motion before she died?" I questioned. "Like a backup plan?"

He nodded. "That would be my guess. All I can tell for sure, is that she wanted you in the dreamworld. The stunt with the sink was to taunt you."

I took in what my dad was saying. "But Nix claimed Alexandria tortured her. She said that she knew information that Alexandria wanted."

My dad smiled softly. "Nix is a compulsive liar. There are many things about her and your grandmother that you are not aware of, but now is not the time for that."

I sighed. I felt like I should have been sad, or angry, or . . . something. I should have at least wanted more information about Nix, but it seemed oddly inconsequential. I shook my head, feeling numb. "Alexandria wanted me to die in the dreamworld, didn't she? I played right into her plan, twice."

He patted my shoulder. "I believe so. I was able to help you the first few times, but I have little power left. In the end, I couldn't save you."

"You were watching the entire time?"

He nodded. "I've been trying to protect you from her, but she's somehow connected herself to you. That connection gave her more power."

I shivered as I tried to come to terms with what he was telling me, and I for some reason remembered the voice that had called out to me. I felt a single tear slip down my face. "Chase found my body, didn't he? I heard him calling out."

My dad nodded again. "He's still with you now. I fear what your grandmother, or even Nix, might do."

"The witches will pull him out of the dreamworld soon," I commented, glad that at least Chase was still alive. "Why did you stop me from running into the light?" I added.

My dad gave me a half smile, but still looked sad. "If you had gone through that gateway, you would have moved on. I wanted to speak with you first."

"It's cold in here now," I observed. "It wasn't before."

My dad nodded. "When you don't move on, you slowly begin to fade. The cold is an unfortunate side effect of that. I've been losing my grasp ever since I arrived in this place. Each time I helped you, I faded a bit more."

I began to cry. "So we're both just going to sit here and fade? Alexandria will win?" I looked down at the dog resting comfortably in my lap. "Did this dog die too, or what?"

"The dog is your guide," he answered, ignoring my first two questions. "He's here to lead you out when you're ready. My guide left me long ago."

I wiped the tears from my face. "Well I'm not going," I stated. "If I'm still real in some way, I can still help my friends. If I'm going down, I'm taking Alexandria with me."

My dad offered me a genuine smile. "You always were stubborn beyond belief."

He stood and offered me a hand up. I gently shoved the dog out of my lap, then took his hand. It felt very real, but also cold, just like mine. I stood and was once again overcome with a feeling of lightness.

"First, show me how to help Chase," I requested. "The witches were going to give us several hours. I don't want anything to happen to him before they pull him out. After that, we'll get Alexandria."

My dad nodded, then closed his eyes. We began to fade out of existence in a cloud of gray smoke. At the last moment, the dog trotted over and butted his head against my free hand. He dissipated with us, then reappeared by my side in the dreamworld.

We stood behind Chase as he shook my dead body, crying and begging me to wake up. I had a feeling he wouldn't be able to see us like we could see him. I went to crouch beside him anyway, placing my hand on his shoulder in an attempt to comfort him.

He whipped around, looking confused, but when his eyes roved over the space I occupied, he looked right through me, then looked back to my dead body.

I followed his gaze. It was strange seeing myself like that. It didn't really bother me for some reason, probably because the whole situation felt somehow fake. Maybe it would feel different once I came to terms with being dead.

The dust in the area had lessened, but still obscured most of the scenery around us. I jumped back as green smoke came into existence near the head of my corpse.

I calmed myself and stood straight as my grandmother appeared before us. My dad came to stand beside me, followed by the dalmatian. The dog let out a low growl as it eyed my grandmother.

She looked down at it with a sneer. Her face was so startlingly similar to my own that it was strange to see her in comparison to my dead body. She wore the same emerald trench coat I'd seen her in when we were both alive.

"You know," she began smugly as she turned her green eyes up to me, "every moment you hang on to this life is another moment I have to hurt the ones you care about."

"I would think in this case you'd want to keep her around," my dad answered for me. "Your hold on her is the only thing giving you power here."

Chase looked over his shoulder directly at us, almost as if he could hear us speaking.

"Xoe?" he questioned.

"Chase!" I exclaimed, elated that perhaps he'd heard or sensed us.

My elation soon subsided as he shook his head and turned back to my body. "I won't leave you here," he whispered. "When the witches pull you out, I'll take you with me."

I felt like I wanted to cry, but wasn't about to give my grandmother the satisfaction. I looked up to see her holding a glowing green sphere of energy in one hand. Her stance was cocky, with her hips jutted to the side and a taunting smile on her face. "He *won't* be leaving here," she said as her smile turned into a grin.

"Why are you so intent on hurting me?" I asked quickly, trying to delay whatever action she might take.

She rolled her eyes. "You *killed me.*"

"Actually I didn't," I corrected, "and even if I did, you tried to kill me first."

She huffed in annoyance. "If you don't move on soon, I *will* kill him."

My dad stepped a little bit in front of me. "Why are you so intent on her moving on?" he asked suspiciously. "She's already dead. What would you stand to gain?"

"Revenge," she said simply, though a nervous shift in her gaze gave away the lie.

"I know you better than that," my dad countered. "You don't waste time on revenge. The only reason you would have gone to all of this trouble is if you had something to gain."

She glanced down at Chase again, then at my body. She held up the glowing sphere in threat, but I almost didn't notice. I was still hung up on the way she'd looked at my body. Almost . . . longingly. I suddenly understood her plan.

"You want my body, don't you? You latched onto it when you died, but you couldn't take it over until I was out of it. You're still trying to complete what you started when we were all alive."

My dad gave me a look of respect for coming to the conclusion before he did, then turned his gaze back to Alexandria. "You need Xoe to move on before you can take over her body, and you're worried that the witches will take that chance away once they summon Chase."

My grandmother's face crumpled, but the moment of weakness was soon washed away by rage. "What does it matter!" she shouted. "You are both dead. The body is no good to either of you, and I will kill the boy if you do not let me have it."

Not ruffled by her outburst in the slightest, my dad went on. "How could you even do this? Possession is only temporary, and should only work on the living."

Alexandria's nerves seemed ready to snap. She glanced down at my body again, and I wouldn't have caught what she was looking at, except for the fact that it was shimmering with red light. The ring. There was something about the ring on my finger that we didn't know.

My dad caught it at the same time that I did. "What did you do?" he asked slowly.

Her lips snapped shut in a tight line. "She was wearing a broken ring," she growled. "I *fixed* it."

"You attached yourself to that ring long before you died, didn't you?" my dad accused.

Alexandria looked smug again as she pushed her long, white-blonde hair behind her shoulder. "One must plan for all contingencies. I knew there was a chance that one of you might kill me. I needed a backup plan."

"Could someone please explain to me what's going on?" I interrupted.

My dad kept his gaze on my grandmother as he replied, "When she fixed your ring, she placed a piece of her soul, or being, or whatever you want to call it into the stone. *That's* what's keeping her in this form, not you. When you summoned a flame in the dust storm, you used *her* magic. That's how it worked. The magic in the ring was too small for you to do anything else."

I attempted to summon a flame into my palm then, and was pleased to see that I still could, even without the ring or my body. I smirked at my grandmother. "And here I'd thought you actually did something nice for me."

"What are you doing?" she asked nervously, glancing at the flame in my palm.

Not wanting to give her a chance to stop me, I threw a ball of fire at my corpse, not caring if I destroyed it as long as I destroyed the ring as well. Alexandria might spare Chase now, but she'd probably kill everyone once she had a body again.

I wasn't even sure if I had the power to burn my corpse, but my dad had more power when he'd first died, maybe I would still have some of mine.

My grandmother threw her energy ball a split

second later. The two forces collided mid-air, and ricocheted off each other. Chase ducked, shielding my corpse from harm. He couldn't see me, but he *could* see my magic.

"Xoe!" he shouted as he sat up, looking around frantically for the source of what had exploded above him.

I looked at my corpse and the offending ring again, then summoned another fireball. This time, Alexandria beat me to the punch and threw a ball of energy directly at Chase.

Not really thinking about my actions, I did the only thing I could think of and threw myself at Chase's crouched form, just as he noticed the energy ball speeding toward him. I kind of went *through* him, but the momentum of my impact was enough to knock him out of the way.

I crouched beside him and thought of the wall of fire I'd summoned the last time we were in the dreamworld. Orange and red flames shot from my upheld palms to envelope us in a fiery bubble.

My grandmother screamed in frustration while my dad stood by helplessly. He'd obviously faded too much to use his magic. "Destroy the ring!" he shouted.

The dalmatian barked furiously outside of the bubble, adding to the chaos of the moment.

I looked around for my corpse, though maintaining our shield took most of my concentration. My eyes finally landed on it, only to find that it was only half inside our bubble. Where my flames met with my skin, they were repelled.

Chase was panting and looking directly at me. "Xoe? How are you here?" he asked in disbelief.

My eyes widened, but I didn't have the concentration to look at him fully. "You can see me?"

I saw him nod out of the corner of my eye.

"Chase," I began trying to keep my voice level and encouraging. "You need to destroy the ring on my body's hand. It's what's keeping my grandmother here."

He looked down at my body. My fire was weakening against my grandmother's onslaught. We were running out of time.

"Hurry," I said through gritted teeth.

He reached forward and quickly took the ring off my hand. We were lucky that it had fallen inside the bubble, else I don't know what we would have done.

He clutched the ring in his fingers and looked down at it. "How do I destroy it?"

"Break the stone!" my dad shouted.

My grandmother turned a look of pure hatred toward him, but quickly looked away to continue chipping away at our shield. I wasn't sure if he had heard my father, or just figured it out for himself, but Chase pointed the ring downward, then thrust his hand toward the earth, slamming the stone on a small rock. The ring's stone cracked open, and my grandmother screamed.

Green light leaked out of the broken stone, just as Alexandria was consumed by the same green glow. The glow condensed into a large sphere as her figure melded and imploded with it. Soon all that was left was a giant, glowing orb. It gave a shudder, then exploded outward, knocking down my shield, then knocking us all onto our backs.

The world went eerily silent as I laid in the dirt, stunned. Then the dalmatian approached and started licking my face. I shoved him off me and sat up. She was gone.

My dad sat up across from me. His grin told me that we'd won.

Chase sat up too, then turned to stare at me in awe.

"You can still see me?" I asked hopefully.

Chase nodded, then looked down at my body. "How are you here?" he asked weakly.

"It would seem Chase inherited some of his father's powers after all," my dad commented as he stood.

Chase looked in my dad's direction like he'd heard him, but it was obvious he couldn't see him.

"You mean he's a Necro-demon like Sam?" I questioned.

"What?" Chase said, returning his gaze to me.

My dad nodded, then suddenly looked sad. "You should tell him goodbye . . . for both of us."

I bit my lip, then looked back to Chase. His dark hair was caked with dirt. His dirt-stained showed dark trails where his tears had fallen.

"I have to go," I said, not knowing what else to say.

His face fell. "You're dead, aren't you?"

I nodded. "You can see me because you have powers just like your brother."

He held out a hand to me, and I took it. His fingers wrapped tightly around mine. "You feel real," he commented. "I feel like . . . " he trailed off as his gaze went distant.

"You feel like what?" I pressed, worried that the witches were already summoning him back to the human world. I still needed to say goodbye.

"Chase-" I began when he didn't answer me, but he raised his free hand to cut me off.

My dad stepped forward, a curious look on his face. "Tell him to pick up the ring," he instructed.

I did as my dad bade, confused about what I was missing.

Chase plucked the damaged ring from the ground and looked down at the broken stone. The dalmatian, who'd been sitting happily by my side, began to bark.

Chase looked in the direction of the dog. "I feel strange. Do you hear something barking?" he asked distantly.

I shook my head, not wanting to take the time to explain. I needed to say goodbye and the witches might summon him any minute.

"Xoe," my dad said evenly as he crouched in front of us, "touch the ring."

I looked at the ring in question. "It's broken."

Chase nodded, thinking that I was speaking to him. My dad gave me an impatient look, reminding me of all the arguments we'd had. Arguments that I missed every day.

I rolled my eyes and reached out a finger toward the ring.

"What are you doing?" Chase questioned.

My finger grazed the broken stone, and my entire body erupted in goosebumps.

My dad looked down at the ring in awe. "It's meant to store souls. I always wondered where its power came from."

I recoiled from the ring. "I don't want to be trapped in there!"

"Touch it again," he said, eyes intent on the ring as Chase stared at me, wondering who I was talking to.

I placed my finger firmly on the ring, annoyed. I was already dead, so I guess I really didn't have much to lose. As soon as my finger touched down I felt a strange pulling sensation, like the ring was taking away a part of me. I waited until the feeling subsided, then met Chase's wide eyes.

"You're more difficult to see now," he said, his voice cracking near the end.

"Tell him to put the ring on your finger," my dad ordered. "Quickly before he gets pulled away."

I held out my hand toward Chase.

"Not *that* finger," my dad corrected, then looked down at my corpse.

I gasped. "Do you think-" I began, but my dad cut me off.

"It's worth a shot," he said quickly.

"Put the ring on my body's finger!" I exclaimed, elated by the implications my dad was making.

Chase didn't even question me. He leaned toward my body and slipped the ring back onto one of my lifeless fingers.

We all paused and stared down at the ring, but nothing happened. My slim hopes dashed, I let out a sob.

Chase turned frantic eyes to me. "I think Cynthia is trying to pull me out!"

My eyes widened. "No," I whispered.

I looked around for something, anything, to stop what was happening, but it was no use. In a last ditch effort, I turned back to Chase. "Break the rest of the ring!" I shouted.

"No!" my dad argued. "It might send you away like it did your grandmother."

I began to cry. "I'm dead anyway!" I shouted back. "I love you!"

Thinking I was talking to him, Chase muttered, "I love you too," then lifted my dead hand to hit what remained of the stone's ring on a rock, just before he disappeared from sight.

16

I had a dream that I was back in the misty cave with my dad, or maybe it wasn't a dream. Maybe my dreams were all reality, but my mind can't fully comprehend what it sees, so it tells me it's all a dream.

We sat together for a long time, with the dalmatian resting his head in my lap. We laughed and reminisced about the short portion of our lives that we'd spent together. Eventually we both grew cold, and my dad announced that it was finally time for him to walk into the light.

"Where will you go?" I asked.

He only laughed at me. "I'm not even sure where *here* is, let alone over *there.*"

I knew he didn't have the answers, but I couldn't just let it drop. "Will I ever see you again?"

He stood and shrugged, then offered me a hand up. "There are always dreams."

I shook my head and began to cry as he helped me stand. "But I never know if they're real. How can I know if I'm really seeing *you*?"

He shrugged again. "As long as they feel real to you, does it matter?"

Before I could answer, he pulled me into a tight hug. "Say goodbye to Chase for me," he whispered in my ear.

"So I'm alive?" I asked, not wanting to pull away from the hug.

"It's time to wake up," he replied, and just like that, I shot up in bed.

I wasn't alone either. Everyone was crammed into my room: Chase, Lucy, Allison, Max, Jason, my mom, and even Devin and Abel.

I took a shuddering breath as I looked around at all of the shocked expressions. I reached to the back of my head where I'd hit the rock. There was dried blood caked in my hair, but no wound.

My eyes lingered on Chase's stunned expression. "How?" I whispered.

He shook his head. "I did what you told me, then I got pulled back here. A few minutes later, you appeared unconscious, but alive, in the middle of the living room."

My mom started to cry, and clung to Abel's arm like he was someone she was actually comfortable with.

"A few minutes . . . " I trailed off. If I'd been in the human world this last bit of time, then my final meeting with my dad really had been a dream.

Something was making snuffling noises beside my bed. I leaned to the side and looked down. The dalmatian was rolling around on the carpet, playing with a stuffed animal.

My eyes widened as I looked back to the people in the room. "Did he appear with me?"

Max, who was standing near the doorway with Allison, answered, "He sure did. Can we keep him?"

I laughed, startling myself. "I don't think I have a choice."

Lucy stepped forward hesitantly, then sat on the bed next to me. She held out a hand, but stopped just short of my shoulder. "C-can I touch you?"

I smiled encouragingly at her. Chase had obviously filled everyone in on what had happened. They were acting like I was still a ghost.

I nodded, almost afraid for her to touch me and shatter the illusion.

Her hand landed solidly on my shoulder, then she pulled me into a tight hug. A moment later, Allison pounced on us, wrapping us both in the circle of her arms. "No more dying allowed," she ordered.

My mom began sobbing anew at that.

After several more minutes of hugging and crying, I looked to Chase to save me from an overwhelming sea of emotion. Plus, I *really* needed to talk to him. He looked to Jason for some reason.

Jason looked strangely worried. "Chase and I need to talk to Xoe," he announced.

Lucy growled at him from her perch on my bed. I patted her shoulder to draw her attention. "I need to talk to them too," I lied. Really I just needed to talk to Chase, but I wasn't going to pass up the opportunity to clear my room of some people.

My mom stepped forward and looked at me with her tear-stained, puffy face like she wanted to say a million different things, but none of them would come out.

"I'm fine," I assured her, "and we're safe now. We left the bad demon girl somewhere in the dreamworld. It's all over."

Her eyes widened at the mention of demon girls and dreamworlds, but she still embraced me in a tight hug, then stepped away and allowed Abel to lead her out of the room. Allison, Max, and Lucy followed. I let out a deep sigh, finally alone in my room with Chase and Jason.

Before I could say anything, Chase blurted out, "We fed you vampire blood."

Whatever I'd been about to say froze on my lips. It took a second for his words to sink in. "You *what?*"

"Um," Chase began, "when I took your coffee to put more creamer in it . . . " he trailed off.

"B-but demons can't be turned into vampires," I stammered.

"But you're half-human," Jason countered.

I looked at him in shock. "Why would you do this?"

"It was our backup plan," Chase cut in. "He gave me a vial of his blood, and if things looked grim enough, I was going to find a way for you to take it. After our dream, I couldn't just go rushing to the dreamworld without a safeguard."

I shook my head, feeling numb and nervous at the same time. "That's why you were so intent on taking my body back. You thought it might reanimate."

He looked down at his feet. "I'm sorry, I just couldn't let you die."

Suddenly I was angry, and it felt a lot better than being hurt, confused, or sad. "I knew the risks going in! That was *my* choice."

Jason's expression was cold. "Would it be the worst thing in the world to be like me?"

"That's not the point," I argued.

He crossed his arms. "Then what is?"

"This is ridiculous," I breathed, utterly perplexed by how the conversation had turned on me. "The point is you two basically drugged me!"

"You're alive," Jason said calmly, "so it won't hurt you any."

I shook my head. "But I *died*. I died with vampire blood in my system. I hope you know what that means, because I sure as heck don't."

Jason bit his lip.

I crossed my arms. "You didn't think of that, did you?"

He opened his mouth to speak, then shook his head. Finally, he met my eyes. "There was only a fifty-fifty chance that it would even work on you, and you were only dead for a short time. You'll be fine."

"Do you know that for sure?" I pressed.

He looked back down, avoiding my eyes.

I looked to Chase. "Did you tell the others?"

He shook his head. "We're the only ones that know."

I sighed. "Don't tell them. There's no need to worry them without reason."

The dalmatian chose that moment to make us aware of his presence by jumping up on the bed with me. He curled up next to me and laid his head in my lap. His dark eyes looked up to meet mine.

"You better not still be trying to lead me toward the light," I scolded.

The dog whimpered, then buried his face in the blanket covering my lap.

I looked up at Chase. "I'm assuming Cynthia pulled Sam out as well?"

He nodded. "Nothing happened to him after we were separated. He was wandering around, lost, when Cynthia and Rose pulled him out."

"Well since he's alive, you better ask him for some

lessons," I replied tiredly, "you might start seeing ghosts from now on."

Chase cringed. "Seriously?"

"Yep," I said as I stroked the dog's head. "You've leveled up. Now both of you get out of my room before I light you on fire."

Neither of them argued with me. They probably didn't believe that I'd light them on fire, but they knew they were wrong. No amount of arguing would change the fact that they had taken my afterlife into their own hands. I couldn't tarry on what changes might happen to me. I'd already been through enough.

I continued to pet the dog as the bedroom door shut behind them. I knew I should go back to the dreamworld to find Nix and take her back to the underground for judgment, but I'd let her fret for a while. The dalmatian yipped happily, as if agreeing with my thoughts.

"I guess you need a name," I said, looking down at my alleged spirit guide.

The dog looked up at me in encouragement.

"Alexondre is dead," I mused, "Alexandria imploded, and nobody wants my terrible name, so how about Alexius? Do you like that?"

The dog yipped again and wagged his tail.

"Alexius it is," I smiled down at him. "You know, I always wanted a dog."

He leapt off the bed and grabbed his stuffed

animal, then returned to my lap happily. I laughed, and was surprised that I still knew how.

There's a lot to be said for the resiliency of humans. Or the resiliency of demons for that matter. Or ghosts . . . or vampires . . . or whatever the heck I was now classified as. The point was that I had lived and died, loved and lost, and I was still the one left standing. Call it luck, or call it resilience. I was still alive, like a cockroach after the apocalypse.

17

I eventually had to face Chase, if only to return him to the underground. Sam had gone on his own with the help of a new collection of ghosts, but Chase refused to go until I talked to him.

It had been my mom that finally convinced me to get the confrontation over with. My friends had left my house, and so had the witches, my new pack members, and Jason. The danger was over with, and everyone else could get on with their lives.

My mom had come into my room shortly after I forced the boys to leave. She was putting on a brave face, but I could tell she was nearing a breakdown. How is a mother supposed to react when her daughter comes back from the dead? I don't think either of us knew. Instead we had talked about the fact that I was still here, and that I had a very upset, sort-of boyfriend waiting downstairs for me. I still would have to give

Jason a piece of my mind, but Chase was the only one waiting around, so he would get a taste of my anger first.

When I finally saw him, I simply held out my hand, anxious to check on Dorrie. He took it. He was still covered in dirt from the dreamworld. His hair was a mess, and he had large bags under his eyes. What stood out the most though, were the tear stains in the dust on his face. He'd wept over my dead body, vowing to bring it home. He'd done whatever he could to keep me alive, and I suddenly wasn't mad at him anymore. What would I have done had the situations been reversed? Would I have fed him vampire blood? I wasn't sure.

We poofed out of existence, then reappeared in my dad's kitchen.

Chase looked over at me, still holding my hand. "I was wondering if it would still work," he commented.

"If what would still work?" I asked, confused.

"Your traveling," he clarified. "Since you could only do it after your grandmother died, I thought it might have just been part of her latching on to the ring."

I pulled my hand out of his and crossed my arms. "So you figured it out, huh?"

"The giant green explosion after I broke the stone kind of clued me in, but I still have a million other questions."

I sighed and looked down at my hands. The ring

didn't show up with my body, and I still didn't understand how I had shown up at all. "So do I," I mumbled.

"Pop Tart!" Dorrie exclaimed as she appeared in the doorway to the entry room.

She rushed toward me like she would swoop me up in an uncomfortable, scratchy hug, but stopped short. She looked me up and down with intelligence radiating in her crystalline blue eyes.

"You seem . . . different," she observed.

"Different?" I questioned, thoughts of vampire blood racing through my mind.

Instead of answering me, she turned and looked at Chase. "You seem different too."

I reached out and patted her shoulder, drawing her attention back to me. "How about we explain everything over pizza?"

Her face lit up, and she trotted off to call for delivery, leaving Chase and I momentarily alone.

He glanced over at me hesitantly, but didn't say anything.

"I'm not mad," I breathed, but didn't have the chance to say anything as he pulled me into a bone-crushing hug.

He pulled away only enough to kiss me, and I let him. In between kisses I managed to get enough air in to say, "But if you ever lie to me again, I'll take you to the dreamworld and leave you there."

He hugged me tightly again, though I could feel

him nod in agreement. "Never again," he whispered against my hair.

I pulled away from him. "And no more plotting with Jason," I added. "I'm still not sure of his motives in this whole situation."

Chase shifted his feet nervously, then looked over his shoulder, as if wishing Dorrie would hurry up and return.

I put my hand on his chin and brought his gaze back to mine. "Didn't we just agree on no more lies? What aren't you telling me."

He inhaled deeply. "Remember when I told you that Jason and I had talked, and everything is fine because he doesn't want to date you right now?"

I nodded, then paused at his word choice. "Wait, what do you mean *right now*?"

Chase grabbed my hand, then pulled me over to the stools at the counter. We sat. "You're aware that Jason is over a hundred years old . . . " he trailed off.

"*And*?" I prompted, eager for him to get to the point.

"And because he's lived a long time," he continued nervously, "he doesn't think like other people."

I drummed my fingers against my knee in impatience. "Go on," I pressed.

Chase sighed in defeat. "You're young," he continued, "and still deciding what you want and who you are."

My jaw dropped as everything clicked into place. "He's waiting for me to change, isn't he?"

Chase shrugged, looking embarrassed.

"And he doesn't care if you date me in the meantime?" I asked, astonished.

"I'm sure he would prefer if we didn't, but he's not going to hate either of us for it. It's not like he doesn't have the time to wait us out."

I shook my head, feeling more confused than ever. "And you're okay with all of this?" I asked skeptically.

Chase grabbed my hand and gave it a squeeze. "If I had my way, I'd have Jason take off, never to return, but I've only been around for twenty-two years, and jealousy is still a prevalent emotion for me."

I narrowed my eyes at him. "So why agree?"

He shrugged. "You broke up with Jason, and now you're sitting here with me, holding my hand. I'm not going to look a gift-horse in the mouth."

I frowned. "Why would he wait for me? I mean, I know we care about each other, but there are plenty of other fish in the sea."

Chase shrugged. "He loves you, and chances are you're immortal, just like him. His only other real option is another vampire, and we've seen how most of them are."

Dorrie chose that moment to come barreling back into the room. "Fifteen minutes!" she exclaimed cheerfully.

One nice thing about demon delivery is that it's fast. I forced a smile for Dorrie, then glanced over at

Chase. "I still find everything you just said incredibly weird."

Chase shrugged. "Sorry?"

I sighed. "I think maybe I should have a talk with Jason. While I think he'll get tired of waiting around sooner rather than later, the idea is still . . . uncomfortable."

Chase gave me a crooked smile. "I don't think it will do any good. Lucy and Allison already tried."

I inhaled too quickly in surprise, sucking saliva into my windpipe. I had to pause for a coughing fit before I could reply, "*What*? Did everyone seriously know about this except for me?"

Chase nodded. "Pretty much. We all said our piece, but he has a pretty good point."

I looked at Dorrie who was watching us with interest, then turned back to Chase. "Which is?"

"He feels sure that you'll live as long as your grandmother and father," he explained, "and he's immortal himself. He doesn't mind waiting us all out, because time is all he has. It's all you have too, if you manage to not get killed . . . again."

I let out a long whistle under my breath. I was *so* not worth a lifetime of waiting. Maybe my friends couldn't convince Jason, but I would still have to try. I didn't believe that I would live forever. I probably wouldn't even last through the year.

I turned to find Dorrie grinning at me.

"What?" I asked tiredly.

She grinned even wider. “Are you part of a love triangle, Dumpling?”

Chase and I both looked at her in disbelief.

“Where on earth did you learn about love triangles?” I asked finally.

She looked down at her feet, seeming almost embarrassed.

Chase answered for her, “She asked for some fiction books a few weeks back. I didn't know what she'd like, so I got a bit of everything, including romance and a few teen books. I'm guessing that's where she picked up *that* term.”

Dorrie nodded excitedly.

I cringed, and was about to answer her when the doorbell rang. I had never been more glad to hear a doorbell in my life. Chase left to answer the door, and when he came back, Dorrie was so excited for pizza that she forgot all about love triangles.

The three of us ate together, and it almost felt like old times again. Times when my dad was still alive, and things were less complicated. These times, of course, were different, but perhaps they weren't as bad as I'd been led to believe.

LATER THAT EVENING, Chase and I left Dorrie to her reading so we could watch a movie in the den. We chose Bram Stoker's *Dracula*, one of my all time favorites.

Chase turned toward me with a smile during one of the slower scenes.

"What is it?" I questioned.

He smiled even wider. "I just realized that we don't have to do anything tomorrow. We can finally just relax."

I smiled back mischievously. "Not quite . . . " I trailed off.

Suddenly Chase looked worried. "What do you mean?"

"My dad told me what he was researching before he died," I admitted.

He pulled back in surprise, but his expression quickly turned to excitement. "I knew I heard his voice! You actually got to talk to him?"

I grinned. "I sure did, and what he had to tell me was a real doozy."

When I didn't elaborate, Chase put his hands on my shoulders and shook me gently. "Spit it out, will ya?" he asked playfully.

I raised an eyebrow and widened my grin. "How do you feel about road trips? We'll need to go somewhere I've never been before."

He looked at the TV screen, then turned back to me and quoted the movie, "I feel myself quite wild with excitement!"

I laughed. "For your sake, Ms. Mina Harker, I hope things turn out better for us than they do for the poor Count."

He sat up straight and lifted his nose in the air. "I always fancied myself more of a Van Helsing."

I patted his hand. "Sorry dear, demons are always the bad guys."

"Says who?" he pouted.

I shrugged. "Everyone, but that's okay. Everyone knows that bad guys have the most fun."

He put his arm around me and turned me to face the TV screen. "Ain't it the truth?" he mused as we sunk into the couch to push our worries aside, if only for a night.

A satisfied smile crossed my face. A little fun seemed like a good idea. If that made me one of the bad guys, then find me a death ray and an eye patch. It was time to embrace my heritage.

ABOUT THE AUTHOR

For more information please visit www.saracroethle.com!

SNEEK PEEK AT BOOK SEVEN!

With one hand on the steering wheel, I held the other toward Chase in the passenger's seat, waiting for him to hand me the coffee he was totally hogging. "Tell me again why we decided to just share a cup?" I questioned.

I caught a glimpse of his smile, his tired dark gray eyes, and his slightly curly black hair, then turned my gaze back to the desolate highway ahead of us. Not that I have anything against Nevada, but it's not the nicest state to drive through, especially midday.

"When we buy two cups you drink all of yours, then move on to mine," he explained for the hundredth time. "This way we keep you from getting over-caffeinated."

"And *no one* wants Xoe over-caffeinated," Lucy added from the seat behind Chase.

"We have bigger problems," Allison groaned from

the seat directly behind me. "Xoe, I think your dog has gas."

We all groaned as the vehicle filled up with a pungent stench. My Dalmatian, Alexius, gave a happy yip from his seat between Lucy and Allison.

"Well you two shouldn't have fed him all of those potato chips," I chided, pushing my way too long blonde hair behind my ear. After an eventful winter spent mostly in the demon underground, my hair had darkened from white-blonde to ash. I was in need of a cut and some sun.

"He came from the spirit world with you when you returned from the dead," Allison countered, "I thought he could handle a few chips."

We all groaned as the car once again filled up with Alexius' stench.

"I think it's time to stop for lunch," I sighed, holding one hand up to cover my nose while I steered with the other.

"Yes please!" everyone else said in unison.

Alexius yipped again excitedly. For a spirit guide, he sure acted like a normal dog. He'd come into my possession when I'd *died* in the dream world. I'd been able to briefly see my father during that time. Alexius had been there to lead my spirit to whatever afterlife might await, but my dad had prevented me from going. We'd basically broken all the rules, and my best guess was that Alexius had nowhere to go after I refused to follow him. Thus, he'd somehow hitched a ride with me back to the real world and physically appeared.

A rest stop with a diner came into view, and I turned on my blinker then exited the highway. As we pulled into the parking lot I saw that the diner, which looked like something out of *Happy Days*, had outdoor seating where we could bring Alexius. Perfect. The weather was nice outside, but I still felt bad making him wait in the car, even if the temperature would be comfortable with the windows rolled down. I'd never been a pet owner before, but I'd turned into one of those annoying people who treat their pets like children. I wouldn't leave a child in the car, therefore I wouldn't leave the dog.

I pulled Allison's new red crossover vehicle into one of many free parking spaces. I had a feeling Allison had only volunteered the vehicle to ensure her presence on our road trip, but it was big enough to fit our luggage and passengers comfortably, and small enough to not kill us on gas mileage, so I'd happily agreed. Plus, it was fun watching her cringe any time we hit a pothole, and she practically screamed any time a branch threatened her shiny red paint job.

I parked and we all piled out of the vehicle. Lucy kept hold of Alexius' neon-green leash, attached to his matching neon collar as we walked across the asphalt to approach the diner. Why neon green? I'd read it was the best way to keep little Alexius from getting hit by a car. It just wouldn't be right to have him go out in such a mundane way after traveling all the way from the spirit world.

Chase took my hand as we walked, sending a little thrill up my bare arm, and not just from the touch. Ever since Chase found out that he could see ghosts, there always seemed to be an extra little zing of other-worldly energy hanging around him, like the ghosts were reaching out for attention. He was doing his best to ignore his newfound gifts, despite his brother Sam's assurances that they'd only get stronger.

I squinted my eyes against the springtime sun, taking a seat at one of the round tables in front of the diner. The tables had large umbrellas to shield them, but I'd ended up in the wrong seat.

Seeing my irritated frown as I blinked up at the sun, Lucy said, "Let's switch tables before Xoe burns the establishment to the ground."

I stood. "I can control my powers very well now, thank you." It was true. I'd been practicing.

We moved to another, more shaded table. I sat, smoothing my khaki shorts under my legs, then Lucy handed me Alexius' leash. Everyone else left me to go inside to order. I trusted Chase to not buy me anything healthy.

With a sigh, I pulled a manilla folder out of my large canvas purse. I'd gone over its contents a million times, but one more couldn't hurt. It was the entire reason for our trip, after all.

I placed the folder on the plastic tablecloth and

opened it, scanning over my dad's research, which was confusing, at best. All I knew was that we were looking for a demon named Art, and I was pretty sure he was my relative. Maybe Art would know why my dad thought I was in danger. Danger that might have had nothing to do with the psychotic ghost of my grandmother.

Lucy and Allison only had one week off school for Spring Break, so we were making a mad dash all the way down to Nevada, taking turns driving throughout the day.

I heard footsteps behind me, then turned to see Allison and Lucy approaching. Of course they'd made Chase wait inside for the food. Lucy placed what looked like iced tea in front of me, then sat with her own drink. She flipped her long, black braid over her shoulder, eyeing the folder on the table.

Allison reached in front of me from the other side and shut the folder as she sat, sipping her drink through a plastic straw. "No more brooding over the info, Xoe. We'll find Art and we'll get some real answers."

"*If* we can find Art," I sighed.

If he'd lived in the underground, like most demons, we could have easily found Art with Sam's help, but he'd left over one hundred years ago, according to what little information Sam had been able to find. Why he left was anyone's guess. He had to have at least a small amount of human blood to leave at all, but that didn't tell me much. There were plenty of half-demons in the world.

Lucy reached over and patted Alexius, who panted happily beside my chair. "Maybe Alexius can sniff him out," she said, grinning down at the dog. She'd bonded much more with Alexius than Allison had.

Allison snorted, then pushed her chin-length, honey blonde hair out of her face. "Yeah, maybe the dog will be good for something after all."

Case in point. Allison had more snide comments for Alexius than she had for *me*, which was really saying something.

"He's good for plenty of things," I argued, taking my turn at patting Alexius' head.

"Like what?" Allison asked. Not waiting for my answer, she pulled her cell phone out of her purse to rapidly type a text.

I looked down at Alexius' happy face and felt an odd mixture of love and sadness. He'd been there the last time I saw my dad, in the spirit world, and had been my comfort in coming to terms with never seeing him again. In many ways, the dog felt like the last piece of my father I had left.

"He's good at being my buddy," I joked, "and that's good enough for me."

Allison sighed and continued texting. Probably talking to Max, who had not been pleased that he couldn't come on our trip. I needed him on another task. It was too soon to entirely abandon my new werewolf pack members, Emma and Siobhan, not that Siobhan really cared. Devin had stayed in Shelby to babysit, and had demanded that at least two other pack members remain behind. Since I wanted Lucy to come more than anyone, Lela and Max were chosen as co-babysitters.

I turned my attention away from Alexius to find Lucy leafing through a text book.

"Hey no homework!" Allison chided, staring at Lucy. "It's Spring Break."

Lucy glanced up from her textbook and rolled her eyes. "*Some* of us want to get into a good college."

Allison frowned and did her signature hair-flip, which was less effective with her now-short hair. "Or you could just stay in Shelby and go to community college with me."

"PSU is only an hour away," Lucy argued. "We could both go and carpool together."

I leaned back in my seat. "Ah for the days where problems were as simple as deciding what college to attend," I mused out loud.

"Oh come on," Allison said, turning her honey-brown gaze to me. "I'd much rather be worrying about the vampire blood in my system and a demon-ey mystery than college."

Lucy scowled. "Way to be blunt, Allison."

"It's fine," I sighed.

Allison was only telling the truth. In all likelihood the vampire blood Jason and Chase had slipped me before I died in the dream world would have no effect. I'd been brought back to life, after all. Chase and my dad had done the same job the vampire blood would have done, except without the added effect of becoming a vampire. Could a demon even become a vampire? I hoped to never find out the answer to that question.

"It's not too late to consider college yourself," Lucy added, turning her gaze to me. "Once you take your GED you can start applying."

I shook my head. "No thanks. It's a demon's life for me."

"See?" Allison said. "Your life is totally better than mine."

"If you say so," I laughed.

Allison was still hell-bent on becoming something other than human. I understood her feeling left out since her two best friends were a werewolf and a demon, and her boyfriend a werewolf too, but I still didn't agree with her. Luckily no one in my pack was willing to make her a wolf, nor was Jason willing to make her a vampire.

The smell of fried food preceded Chase's arrival. He placed a tray on the table filled with baskets of french fries, two burgers, chicken strips, and a grilled cheese with a ridiculous amount of pickles on the side. He removed the grilled cheese plate and placed it in front of me.

"You really do know the way to my heart," I

commented, looking down at the exact meal I would have wanted had I thought to ask for it.

He smiled as he took his burger plate. "Or at least the way to your stomach."

Lucy took the other burger plate, and Allison the chicken.

Alexius whined, and we all turned as one to look at Allison.

She glared at us.

"You know Alexius *loves* chicken strips," I pressed.

She bowed her head in defeat, then handed me one of her chicken strips to feed to the dog. "And you guys wonder why I don't like him," she muttered.

Alexius didn't seem to catch her rude comment, and gladly accepted the chicken strip.

The rest of us dug into our food. Just four normal friends and a dog on a road trip. Anyone looking at us wouldn't think twice.

If only they knew the truth.